JUST A LITTLE
HOOKUP

Carly Phillips

Erika Wilde

JUST A LITTLE HOOKUP

Being a bachelor has its perks. It also has its downside. Just ask Derek Bettencourt.

Standing on stage and being auctioned off in the name of charity is awkward AF... until his business partner's younger sister wins him for the weekend. He's all hers to do with as she pleases and he can't say he's unhappy with the prospect. Especially since she saved him from an ex-fiancée determined to get her claws into him again.

Jessica Cavanaugh never intended to bid on the man she's had a lifetime crush on. But her spur-of-the-moment decision gives her a chance to exact a bit of playful payback, for old time's sake. And Derek is all too happy to indulge Jessica's whims.

What starts as a fun, flirty, game, with Derek acting as her personal handyman, quickly turns into a steamy and *forbidden* weekend. Lines are crossed that they never intended and emotions unravel their playful facades. Afterward, he can't get the gorgeous, full-figured woman out of his head and he's determined to make her his.

But how can they concentrate on a future when someone is threatened by their relationship and will do anything to come between them?

Chapter One

"See anything you like?"

Jessica glanced from the larger-than-life poster featuring photos of the bachelors up for auction at tonight's charity event to her best friend, Avery, who wore a knowing smile.

Jessica shrugged nonchalantly. "Twelve gorgeous single men up for auction. What's not to like?"

"Let me be more specific," Avery said, as other guests strolled along the adjoining tables near them, filled with items up for silent auction. "Is there anyone in *particular* you'd like?"

Jessica knew which bachelor Avery was

alluding to. Dark-haired, green-eyed Derek Bettencourt, her secret crush since she was a teenager. He was also her older brother Ben's best friend and business partner. If that little detail didn't make him off-limits, there were two other very legitimate reasons why her attraction to him would never be reciprocated.

One, she wasn't his type at all.

And two, he'd only ever treated her like a second little sister.

Unfortunately, her infatuation with the man was stronger than ever.

"I am not bidding on anyone tonight," she insisted, finishing off her third glass of champagne for the evening and enjoying the pleasant buzz she was feeling. She'd already supported the charity in other ways . . . the per-plate fee for attending and even bidding on a few silent-auction items that interested her.

"No?" Arms crossed over her chest, Avery tapped her chin thoughtfully with her finger, a devious look twinkling in her eyes. "You know, this might be the perfect opportunity for you to get a little payback."

Jessica tipped her head in confusion. "What are you talking about?"

"Remember that summer our senior year when Derek blabbed about us sneaking out of the house and going to that party where we got drunk and stoned?"

Ten years had passed, but it was hard to forget any of the painful, humiliating things that had happened that last year of high school. Or the party they'd stupidly gone to, thinking that being around the cool kids and doing the same stuff they did would make them fit in. They never had— all because they were the chubby chicks none of the popular girls wanted to be seen with.

Instead, she and Avery had been the target of ridicule on a regular basis. At least they'd had each other.

"He didn't really blab," Jessica said, automatically defending Derek, since he'd been the one they'd called for a ride home from the party. "I mean, it wasn't his fault that my mother overheard him telling my brother what we did." Which resulted in her being punished for her antics.

"Still, you spent *two weeks* grounded and doing ridiculous chores, which meant you missed out on being with *me* at the lake house for the rest of the summer."

The yearly vacation with Avery had been the one thing she'd been looking forward to, and her mother had known it. "Yeah, that part sucked."

"Just saying," Avery teased. "You could put him to work around your new place. Make him paint the fence or trim the hedges . . . shirtless. Watching all that sweat drip down his chest and into the low waistband of his shorts as he labored away on your . . . shrubbery."

Jessica's face flamed at the hot, sexy images of Derek now emblazoned in her mind, even if she knew Avery was just trying to play match-maker in her own not-so-subtle way. "Okay, you can stop now. It's not going to happen."

As much as she'd enjoy having Derek's undivided attention for a weekend, it would also be nothing short of sheer torture. Ogling but not being allowed to touch.

"Jessica!" a female voice called out.

She turned around to see Faith Dare approaching. Jessica had been introduced to Faith through her brother's friendships with the Dare siblings, and the other woman was becoming one of Jessica's best Curvy Girl Couture customers.

Jessica took in the red sequin mermaid-style gown Faith wore, the one Jessica had designed especially for her voluptuous curves and fuller figure. "You look amazing."

"Don't I, though?" Faith asked with a laugh and did a little spin that made her long, blond hair fall around her bare shoulders. "You outdid yourself with this custom dress. I was lucky that Jason let me leave the house tonight," she said of her hunky husband. "He took one look at me and got that seductive gleam in his eyes. It's been like that all evening, so it's going to be a very good night when we get home, if you know what I mean."

Jessica loved seeing Faith's elevated confidence. Making women like herself feel beautiful in their own skin was all she'd ever wanted and why she'd created her own fashion line for females who loved their curves, which she sold in her boutique and online.

"By the way, the desserts you made for this evening were to die for," Jessica said, complimenting the other woman right back. Faith ran her own successful business, Faith's Sweet Treats, which were incredible.

"Oh, my God," Avery cut in with a little orgasm-like moan. "I need those cheesecake brownie bars in my life on a daily basis."

Faith laughed. "Thank you. I was thrilled when Aurora asked me to cater the desserts. Hasn't she done a fabulous job with this event?"

"Yes, she has. It's impressive," Jessica replied, glancing around the grand ballroom located in the Meridian NYC hotel, an upscale establishment owned by the Dare family. There were at least one hundred guests who'd attended the charity event, hosted by Aurora Dare—another woman connected to the Dare family by marriage—whose nonprofit, Future Fast Track for foster kids, would benefit from the influx of donations tonight.

It was a charity Jessica had a personal attachment to, since she'd been diagnosed with polycystic ovary syndrome as a teenager. Knowing that she might not be able to have kids of her own as a result of PCOS, she'd already considered the possibility of adopting or fostering a child one day.

An announcement came over the speakers that the bachelor auction would be starting in thirty minutes, and after finishing up their conversation with Faith, Jessica and Avery headed to the ladies' room to freshen up.

She was still enjoying her happy, tipsy state as they walked into the lounge—complete with velvet-cushioned chairs, couches, and mirrored vanities—until she heard a familiar, *grating* voice drifting from the adjoining partitioned area, where the bathrooms and sinks were located. The running water indicated someone was washing their hands.

Jessica stiffened, immediately knowing who the voice belonged to. Her high school nemesis, Claire Sutherland. The rich mean girl who'd made her life miserable back then, and the catty woman who still had an air of entitlement about her now. Not to mention, she'd once been Derek's fiancée—a fact that left an unpleasant taste in Jessica's mouth.

Her stomach gave a little twist, and when Avery mouthed to her, *Do you want to go?*, Jessica shook her head and stepped up to one of the mirrors. She hadn't had any contact with Claire yet this evening, but now that they were in the same space, she refused to let the other woman run her off.

She wasn't that insecure teenager any longer. Jessica had done a lot of growing and self-reflecting since graduating high school, even if Claire had not. Ten years later, and Claire was still shallow and judgmental. Though to your face, she tried to pretend she was all sweetness and sugar, her real self eventually showed through. Jessica had been the target of Claire's teenage cruelty, but she refused to let the other woman intimidate her now.

The water shut off, and then came the sound of paper towels rustling, as Claire continued to speak. "If Derek refuses to take my calls or answer my texts, winning him at this bachelor auction for an entire weekend will definitely get his attention. I know he's upset about what . . . happened, but I just need the chance to make it up to him."

Jessica couldn't ignore that slight pang in her chest when she thought about Derek and Claire having been together. *That* had been a tough pill to swallow, and she couldn't imagine what Derek had seen in the other woman

beyond the physical—though at least he'd come to his senses eventually and ended their engagement. Clearly, Claire wasn't taking the breakup very well, even though it had happened well over six months ago.

Jessica pulled out her lipstick just as Claire's best friend, Peyton, spoke.

"How do you think he'll react when you tell him you're taking him to our ten-year high school reunion so you can flaunt the fact that you snagged yourself a billionaire?" the equally mean girl asked.

"He doesn't need to know that last part," Claire said dismissively. "And he won't have a choice in the matter once I win him and he's mine for a weekend. I can't show up without him." She sounded desperate.

In the mirror, Jessica exchanged a glance with Avery, who rolled her eyes at Claire's dramatics.

"Well, you *could* show up without Derek," Peyton said. "But considering you've told most of our friends that you're getting back together with him and you've already RSVP'd, adding him as your plus-one, yeah, it would look bad if you arrived solo."

9

"It's not going to happen," Claire said resolutely. "Once I win him at tonight's auction and we spend a weekend together, he'll realize that I made a silly little mistake and I'm perfect for him."

"Both of your mothers will be thrilled if you reconcile. After all, they're the ones who wanted you two together in the first place."

Avery made a gagging motion with her finger in her mouth, and Jessica stifled a laugh. From what she'd learned from her brother, Derek's ambitious mother had wanted her son married into another influential family and had gone so far as to orchestrate the relationship. Though Ben had never divulged what *silly little mistake* had prompted Derek to break things off.

"Exactly. At least—" Claire stopped abruptly as they came around the corner, belatedly realizing that they weren't alone. "Oh, hey ... hi, Jessica."

Jessica didn't miss the way the other woman gave her formfitting gown a flagrant once-over, her quick sneer intended to make Jessica doubt herself. But even Claire couldn't put a dent in how confident Jessica felt in the

sexy gown she'd designed—one that accentu-ated her breasts and hips and made her feel like a million bucks. Like she'd thought earlier, she had come a long way since high school.

"Hi, Claire. Peyton," Jessica replied, not bothering to turn around, though she could see both women behind her in the mirror.

"I don't suppose the two of you are going to our ten-year reunion next month?" Claire asked, knowing that they'd most likely over-heard the conversation she'd just had with Peyton. Before Jessica or Avery could reply, Claire waved a dismissive hand. "Oh, you're probably not going. I know you don't have the greatest high school memories."

The other woman's tone was sugary sweet. As if she felt bad, when in reality, Claire was the reason for their crappy experience. While most people might have grown up in the past ten years and apologized for their behavior, Claire wasn't that person. She still wore that air of superiority like a designer dress.

Jessica dropped her lipstick into her purse, snapped it shut, and finally turned around. "Actually, I have no desire to go. I have nothing to prove to our classmates." *Unlike you,* she wanted to add, but knew it was implied, considering Claire was trying to shore up her appearance by winning Derek tonight. "Besides, I already keep in touch with anyone who matters to me."

Claire's eyes flashed with something akin to anger. "Or maybe you don't want to go, knowing that Derek, your teenage crush, will be there with *me*?" Her expression turned smug.

Unfortunately, Claire knew Jessica's secrets. Like most young girls, she'd made the mistake of writing her thoughts and dreams in a notebook, including her infatuation with Derek —which Claire had stolen and used to embarrass her—in school and on social media. It was no shock that Claire would use the dig now as an attempt to divert them from the fact that they'd just overheard Claire's plan to *buy* Derek. So if he *did* go to the reunion with her, it wouldn't be of his own free will.

At least that knowledge gave Jessica a small bit of pleasure.

Ignoring the snide remark, Jessica kept her composure and gave Claire a tight smile. "No matter who you end up going with, I'm sure you'll have a great time."

She and Avery walked out of the lounge, and Jessica didn't realize just how tense she was until Avery touched her arm and said, "Take a deep breath. You're better than her. We both are and you proved that in there."

Jessica did as her friend suggested and pulled in a long breath, then let it out slowly.

"And just for the record," Avery said, "Claire doesn't have to be the one to win Derek tonight."

Jessica blinked, letting that thought settle inside her, but ultimately, she shook her head. "Nope." Snagging another glass of champagne from a passing tray, she squared her shoulders as they walked toward the staging area where the auction would be held. "I'm not going to stoop to her level and get into a bidding war over a man."

What did they say about famous last words?

Chapter Two

Derek Bettencourt glanced around the ballroom, preparing himself for the inevitable auction that would start soon. He was surrounded by at least one hundred guests who'd attended the charity gala to support Aurora Dare's event, and it didn't escape his notice that many of them were wealthy single women hoping to win a three-day weekend with a well-off bachelor from the upcoming Most Eligible Bachelors of New York City event.

And he was one of the suckers about to be put on display.

When the after-dinner musicians left the stage and a few people started rearranging

things to prepare for the auction, D॰
his head and mock-glared at his sist
who was responsible for getting him
situation.

"I can't believe you talked me into tl
said, growing more uncomfortable a:
bidding time neared. "Or should I
pressured?"

Nikki smiled sweetly, looking stunning i॰
shimmering beige gown that emphasized h॰
modelesque figure. "You know you can'
resist me."

She spoke the truth. His sister was young
and beautiful and knew how to wrap him, and
her new fiancé, Asher Dare, around her finger.
Yeah, Derek would do just about anything for
Nikki, just to see her happy after everything
she'd been through lately, though Asher was
doing a fine job of that these days.

His sister absolutely glowed—which made
it easier for Derek to accept that Asher—who
was twelve years older than Nikki—had made a
move on his sister. Considering his friend had
put a ring on Nikki's finger and both of them
looked annoyingly smitten with one another, it

was difficult to hold that lapse in judgment against his friend.

"Your sister can be incredibly persuasive," Asher chimed in from beside Nikki. He wore a smirk on his face, which told Derek the jerk was enjoying his discomfort way too much.

"I'm well acquainted with her feminine wiles," he replied, while his sister merely batted her lashes at him oh-so-innocently. "It would have been easier for me to just write a sizeable check for the nonprofit."

"But not nearly as much fun," Asher said, his eyes alight with amusement—a lighthearted side that Nikki brought out in him. "It's not often I get to see you squirm."

If they weren't surrounded by high society, Derek would have told his friend to *politely* fuck off.

"It's for a good cause," Nikki piped in, looping her arm through Asher's.

"I'm not refuting that." Derek slipped an index finger between the tight collar of his dress shirt and his throat and gave it a tug. The damn tuxedo bow felt as though it was tightening around his neck like a noose. "I'm just a little leery of who I might end up with and

what she'll want out of her three days with me."

"Maybe a little stud service?" Asher joked.

Nikki smacked Asher on the chest. "Behave," she scolded him. "Not all women are sex-crazed."

A slow smile curved Asher's mouth as he gazed at his fiancée, and Derek grimaced as he read between the lines of that *look*. "Jesus Christ, I do not need to know those things about my sister."

Nikki blushed, then quickly changed the subject. "By the way, did you happen to see who is here tonight?"

The way his sister wrinkled her nose in distaste told him exactly to whom she was referring. "Yes."

His ex-fiancée, Claire Sutherland—who gave new meaning to the phrase *dodged a bullet*. He'd ended things with her a little over six months ago, but that hadn't stopped Claire from trying to mend a relationship that was, quite frankly, unfixable. There were just some lies and deceit a person couldn't overlook.

"I'm sure she's here to find herself some fool who is blinded by nothing more than her pretty face." As soon as the words were out of her mouth, Nikki gave him a pained, apologetic look and quickly added, "No offense."

"None taken," he said and meant it. As difficult as it was to admit, even to himself, he had been Claire's fool at one time, until he'd discovered she was all beauty and no substance. He'd later learned she'd even said some shitty things about Nikki and her modeling career behind her back. Badmouthing his sister was also unforgivable. "As long as she leaves me alone, that's all I care about."

So far, he'd managed to avoid her by keeping to the opposite side of the ballroom or staying in groups of people, but he didn't know how long that reprieve would last. Since their breakup, Claire had been calling and texting, telling him how sorry she was for everything that had happened, asking for a second chance, and swearing to him that she'd changed. That what she'd done wasn't really that bad in the scheme of things . . .

Hell, even his own mother was pressuring him to give Claire a second chance. Then again, Collette Bettencourt always had ulterior motives for everything she did, and it was usually to elevate her and his father's social or political standing. Hence, his mother's desire to see him marry a woman from a wealthy family who was a major donor to his father's potential, and very likely, presidential campaign.

Sure, Derek believed anyone could change, but once burned, twice shy and all that. Not only did he not trust Claire but he didn't like her as a person—no matter how much she professed she'd learned from past mistakes.

"So, how did your partner get out of being a participant in the bachelor auction?" Asher asked, snapping Derek out of his unpleasant thoughts.

"Ben's out of town on a business trip, the lucky bastard," Derek said jokingly.

Ben Cavanaugh was his longtime friend and business partner in Blackout Media, a conglomerate company that dealt in mergers and acquisitions of failing media enterprises and turned them into multi-billion-dollar businesses. They'd started the firm during their time together in business school and had built it into a major contender in the industry.

"I did see that Jessica is here," Nikki said, mentioning Ben's sister. Jessica and Ben had grown up a few houses down from Derek and Nikki in the same upscale neighborhood. But eight years separated the women, so while they were now friendly, they'd never attended the same school, their age gap too far apart.

Derek nodded. "I talked to Jessica briefly during the cocktail hour." And he'd been seated at the table across from her during dinner.

She'd been within his line of sight and he'd watched her throughout the meal, his dick hardening in a way that would make her brother want to kick his ass.

She'd smiled and laughed in conversation with her best friend, Avery, her expressions animated, her green eyes bright, with a sassy quirk to her red lips. Growing up, Derek hadn't thought of Jessica as anything more than his best friend's little sister. Mostly, she'd been a pain in their ass, and as he and Ben had gotten older, Derek had even felt as protective of Jessica as he did of Nikki. But over the past few years, he'd watched her blossom from an uncertain, vulnerable girl into a beautiful woman.

She'd really come into her own, as an independent, successful, and most importantly, *confident* female, and he couldn't help but see her in a different light. Now, she embraced what had once made her so insecure and fucking owned that part of herself, and he found that bold and daring determination she exuded sexy as hell. Not that he'd ever let Ben know the truth. That when Derek looked at Ben's sister these days, he couldn't help but wonder what her long, silky blonde hair would feel like wrapped around his fist, or what her smooth skin tasted like, or the sounds she'd make in the throes of orgasm, or how he'd like to shut up that sassy mouth of hers with a hot, deep kiss. . .

Yeah, totally not cool. Not cool at all.

"Earth to Derek," Asher said, snapping a finger in front of his face. "Damn, this auction must really have you psyched out." He shot Derek a sympathetic look. "While you're mentally preparing yourself to be sold, I'm going to let your sister deal with you while I go enjoy a drink with Linc and Beck at the bar. I'll bet Beck is laughing his ass off at his brothers being a part of the auction, too."

At least Derek would be able to commiserate on stage with Tripp and Drew while they stood on display. Aurora had deemed them all single, eligible, and therefore, "man candy catnip" for the auction.

"You go do that," Derek muttered, eager to not be the brunt of Asher's jokes.

Nikki let out a chuckle. "Go," she said to her man, patting his shoulder.

Asher leaned down and kissed her full on the lips before striding off, Nikki gazing after him.

Derek yanked at his too-tight collar again and his sister playfully smacked his hand away. "Stop being so anxious. You're making your tie crooked," she chided. She straightened the bow and sighed, lifting her gaze to his. "You know, this really isn't such a bad thing."

He arched a brow. "What, being auctioned off like cattle or spending a weekend with a woman, whether we get along or not, just because she's the highest bidder?"

"It could be fun." She gave him a dazzling smile. "Or you might even be bought by the woman of your dreams and you just don't know who she is yet."

He rolled his eyes so hard he almost hurt himself. "Clearly, you still have your fanciful head in the clouds when it comes to romance. The last thing I'm looking for is love."

Nikki smoothed a hand down his tuxedo jacket lapel, a knowing look in her eyes. "That's usually when it finds you. I mean, look at me and Asher. Total opposites and totally unexpected. Who would have thought Mr. Grumpy Pants would be all warm and mushy on the inside? If you hadn't thrown us together on his island, we probably never would have realized how perfect we are for each other."

He smiled. "I'm happy for you. Really."

"And that's all I want for you. The same kind of happiness." She paused a moment, then continued. "Considering everything that's happened in our family as of late, it would be nice to see you settled, too."

He couldn't disagree with the family part of her comment. Just recently, Nikki had called their mother out on her controlling and abusive behavior, which hadn't gone over well. She'd then announced her decision to quit modeling and pursue her own dreams and not be their mother's puppet any longer. Derek was incredibly proud of his sister for standing up for herself, but when he added in his own recent breakup with Claire, there was no denying the tension within their family. With all her wishes thwarted, their mother was being an absolute bitch about, well, pretty much everything—because both her children had disappointed her in different ways.

"I'm perfectly happy," he assured his sister. "Just because our family is shit doesn't mean that my life is, too."

"But it would be so much better with a special someone in it," Nikki persisted. "And not just one of your random hookups."

"They're not random."

"Oh, yeah, I forgot," she said with a small amount of sarcasm. "You have at least half a dozen women on speed dial."

His answer was a smirk, in hopes that she'd drop the subject.

Of course she didn't let it go. "You know, those women you hook up with are hoping for something more."

"And I've made it perfectly clear that all I'm interested in is a good time," he replied, not even close to being ready to dive back into the dating pool. "They know the rules and what to expect."

She frowned at him. "I just don't want you to turn into a thirty-two-year-old manwhore."

He laughed. "Yes, God forbid that should happen."

The sound of someone tapping a microphone three times had everyone's attention turning toward the stage, where Aurora stood at a podium. She was five months pregnant and glowed in a deep purple gown that complemented her blond, upswept hair and highlighted the subtle diamonds around her neck and hanging from her ears. Nick, her husband, stared adoringly from the stage. No, Derek thought, he was in no way ready for *that*.

"Single ladies, gather around," she encouraged the women. "It's time to meet some of the Most Eligible Bachelors of New York City! As for the gentlemen who are part of the auction, will you take your place on the stage behind me, please?"

Leaving his sister, Derek made his way up to his designated spot. There were twelve small circles on the floor in numerical order, and he stepped up to the number four. Drew stopped beside him as number five, followed by his brother, Tripp, as number six in the lineup.

While the rest of the guys settled into their places, Derek glanced at Drew. "So, how'd you get suckered into this?" he asked in a low voice.

"Chloe, of course," he grumbled of his brother Beck's wife, even though there was affection for her in his gaze. "She adores Aurora and begged us to be a part of the auction."

From what Derek recalled, Aurora had been homeless before her rightful family, the Kingstons, found out she even existed. Now, she was Chloe's sister.

"Well, there's no denying a doctor and a lawyer ought to be a nice draw for the ladies bidding," he joked as he pointed out Drew's and Tripp's professions.

Drew's mouth lifted in a half grin. "Says the billionaire media mogul."

Derek chuckled. "Fair enough."

Once all the bachelors were in place, Aurora addressed the group of women standing in front of the stage. "Now, I'm sure you've all had a chance to look through the booklet and read each bachelor's profile to pick out just the right man for your weekend enjoyment," she teased. "Open up those wallets for a worthy cause and let the bidding begin!"

Aurora stepped down from the stage and an older gentleman took her place at the podium to conduct the auction. He called up the first bachelor, started the bidding at ten thousand and while a few single ladies upped the ante on the guy, Derek took the opportunity to gauge the small crowd.

His ex-fiancée, Claire, was hard to miss, standing in the front wearing a slinky emerald-green gown with thin straps and a low-cut bodice that deliberately flaunted her surgically enhanced breasts. Her dark hair was swept up in some kind of complicated style, and her makeup was dark and dramatic. He couldn't deny that she was *outwardly* gorgeous, and he did his best not to make eye contact with her.

Standing on the opposite side of the group, Jessica was equally difficult to overlook in a black shimmery gown. The short sleeves fell off her shoulders, drawing a man's eyes—*his eyes*—to the neckline that dipped just enough to show a tasteful amount of cleavage. Whereas Claire's breasts were firm silicone, Jessica's looked full and soft and *real*. As were the rest of her curves. The dress teasingly outlined her waist and shapely hips, but it was the daring thigh-high slit that captured his attention. With the barest shift in her stance, the material gave him a glimpse of her leg and the bright red designer heels that made a bold, head-turning statement.

She looked sinfully seductive, with her softly curled blonde hair flowing around her shoulders. She wore just enough makeup to enhance her features, not overpower them. Soft and subtle, except for those red-painted lips that had him conjuring a few dirty fantasies of seeing that lipstick smeared along the length of his cock.

He swallowed back a groan and flicked his gaze back up to her eyes. She'd caught him looking at her—or maybe he'd caught her looking at him—and she gave him a smile before her best friend, Avery, said something that diverted her attention. He saw Jessica glance toward Claire and was surprised to see a disdainful look in his ex's eyes, directed straight at Jessica.

What the hell was up with that?

While all this was happening, the first bachelor sold for twenty-two thousand, the second one for eighteen thousand, and the third, an even twenty grand.

Then it was Derek's turn, and he stepped forward and pasted a smile on his lips—rather than a grimace—while the auctioneer did a quick introduction, summing up the profile written in the brochure most of the women had in their hands.

"Who will start the bidding at ten thousand dollars for a three-day weekend with Derek Bettencourt?" the gentleman asked, as he had for every bachelor that had stood in the same spot before Derek.

"I'll bid fifty thousand dollars!" a familiar voice called out.

Derek turned his head and looked at the source of the voice, his stomach churning. Claire gave him a smug smile, obviously certain that no one would top that bid. And she was probably right. Which meant he would be stuck with his ex for three entire days.

Well, fuck.

Chapter Three

Jessica had sworn she wasn't going to bid on a man at the bachelor auction, and especially not on Derek, and she'd meant those words at the time. But after a few glasses of champagne and Claire's rude comments still swirling in her mind, topped off by that smug look her nemesis gave Derek when she placed her outrageously high opening bid, certain no one would provide competition, Jessica was tempted to do something a little rebellious and prove to that bitch she couldn't have everything she wanted.

But none of those things were what changed Jessica's mind. It was the panicked look that flashed across Derek's features. A feeling she knew all too well—being cornered by someone you didn't like, with no escape. Of being forced to do something you dreaded. And clearly, Derek did not want to spend a weekend with his ex-fiancée.

"Seventy-five thousand!" Jessica blurted out, startling even herself. But once the words were spoken, she knew she was in it to win the auction and Derek. There was no backing out now.

The women around her gasped in shock. Up on the stage, Derek's brows rose in surprise at her—clearly, he hadn't expected any other bids and certainly not from her—and when Jessica dared to glance at Claire, the other woman's glare was sharp as daggers.

Jessica held back a grin. Yeah, payback was a bitch sometimes, and just the thought of Claire going to the reunion without the man she'd added as her plus-one, for the sole purpose of flaunting him to her friends, was going to be sweet, indeed.

"Eighty thousand!" Claire shouted at the auctioneer, her tone on the verge of being desperate.

"One hundred thousand," Jessica countered calmly, smiling and keeping her eyes on Derek, who appeared both grateful and amused by her decision to bid on him.

She could keep topping Claire's amount all night long. She had a ridiculous trust fund from her grandparents she rarely touched, the money would go to a good cause, and for once she actually had the upper hand over Claire, and she couldn't deny that leverage felt amazing.

Tonight, Claire was going to learn that just because she desired something, it didn't mean it was just going to fall into her lap.

"Holy shit," Avery whispered gleefully. "Claire looks like she's going to have a coronary."

Jessica casually sipped from her champagne flute, refusing to look at the other woman, but she could only imagine how much she was fuming.

"One hundred twenty-five thousand dollars," Claire said, the words sounding as though they'd been spoken through gritted teeth.

Another round of gasps echoed in the ballroom, and everyone glanced expectantly at

Jessica, waiting to see if she raised the bid or folded.

Again, very calmly, like she had all the time and money in the world, she said, "One hundred fifty thousand dollars."

It was an insane amount of money—insane enough that Claire must have realized Jessica wasn't going to back down or opt out, because the ballroom went quiet as the auctioneer did his *going once, going twice, going three times* spiel. When no one countered, he slammed his gavel down and gestured toward where Jessica stood in front of the stage.

"Derek Bettencourt, sold to the beautiful woman in the black dress," the gentleman in the tuxedo said jovially. "Thank you for your very generous donation. You can meet your bachelor over in the greeting area just outside the ballroom."

"Oh, my God, Claire just stormed off and she looks pissed," Avery said, keeping Jessica apprised of their nemesis's whereabouts. "I wonder if this is the first time something hasn't gone her way."

"Probably." The two of them headed toward the double doors leading out of the ballroom. "I doubt she's familiar with any form of humiliation, so I'm sure this loss knocked her off her game."

Avery snickered. "Ahh, it really is true what they say about revenge being sweet."

As they passed the bar area, Jessica swapped out her empty champagne glass for a fresh one, needing the liquid fortitude to face her secret crush. "Since I have to meet with Derek, I'll come find you after we're done discussing things."

"You're going to do him, aren't you—I mean, do *it*," she amended, with a naughty gleam in her eyes at her double entendre. "You know, putting him to work around your place?"

"Of course," Jessica drawled, knowing her friend meant something else entirely. "What else would I do with him for a whole weekend?"

"Oh, Jessica." Avery's sigh was filled with feigned disappointment. "Do I really have to give you a list of all the ways that man could fulfill every single dirty fantasy you've ever had of him?"

Her cheeks heated with a telltale blush. "Derek doesn't see me like that."

"Maybe that's because you've never given him a reason to. A whole weekend, under your roof, at your beck and call. Your every wish granted, so to speak." Avery grinned. "You know, you could model the new Curvy Girl Couture Lingerie line for him and get his opinion on the different outfits."

Jessica laughed. "You're incorrigible. And the designs are already set for the launch next month, so his opinion isn't going to matter."

Avery shook her head, a hopeless look in her eyes. "Do you really have so little imagination or sense of adventure?"

"I'm being a realist here, Avery," she said with a shrug. "No matter how I might feel about Derek, all he and I will ever be is friends."

"With benefits?" Avery waggled her brows.

Jessica rolled her eyes at her friend. "And on that note, I'm heading out to the greeting area. I'll be back in a little bit."

She left before Avery could say anything more. As she approached the lounge that had been set up for the auction couples to meet up, she saw Derek already standing there with the other men and women who'd been paired up before him.

His tailored tuxedo fit his broad shoulders and lean form flawlessly, and as she walked closer, she was very aware of the appreciative way he looked at her. His eyes skimmed across her breasts and slowly perused their way lower, to the thigh-high slit in her dress, then all the way down to the red heels she wore, his gaze seemingly lingering longer than a friendly or brotherly glimpse.

Or maybe that was just wishful thinking on her part, she mused, taking a drink of her champagne. Regardless, that illusion made her feel desirable, so she pretended, in her mind, that maybe there had been something more to his eyeing her.

When she finally reached him, he took her free hand, stepped up to her, and brushed his warm lips across her cheek in greeting like he'd done a hundred times before. Affectionate but always chaste, and every time, Jessica fantasized about turning her head at the last second so his lips touched hers, just to see what would happen. Despite gaining confidence over the years, she wasn't *that* brazen.

Derek stepped back and smiled at her. "I should have told you earlier that you look beautiful tonight."

The compliment, coming from him, was everything. "Thank you. You look very handsome yourself." An understatement. The man was sexy as sin, drop-dead gorgeous, and no matter how good she felt about herself these days, way out of her league.

He looked down at himself, then back at her, a playful gleam in his eyes. "What, this old thing?"

She laughed, enjoying the fact that they were so at ease with one another. There was no awkward getting-to-know-you phase like the other two couples seemed to be engaged in.

Derek tipped his head, his vivid green eyes regarding her curiously. "So, you know I have to ask . . . why did you do that?"

"You mean why did I bid on you?" she clarified.

"Uh, yeah, in the amount of *a hundred and fifty thousand.*"

She shrugged and downed the rest of the bubbly liquid in her crystal flute. "I guess you could blame it on the champagne."

He smirked as he took the empty glass from her fingers and set it aside. "You should have learned long ago that you don't make the best decisions while intoxicated, Ms. Cavanaugh," he teasingly reminded her. "But regardless, I owe you, big-time."

"Oh, yes, you do," she agreed in a subtle tone. He was referring to Jessica saving him from Claire, while she had a fun little payback in mind.

"Can I at least help cover the donation?" he asked.

She shook her head. "Thank you for the offer, but no. I knew what I was doing and how much I could afford to spend."

He shoved his hands into his pants pockets. "Well, thank you seems inadequate, considering the alternative that was waiting for me." He winced at what he'd narrowly avoided.

"Oh, don't worry. I'll get my money's worth," she said, just mischievous enough to leave him wondering. "Want to know what I saved you from?"

A pained look passed across his handsome features, and he tugged at the bow tie securing the collar of his shirt. "A nightmare weekend with my ex?"

"Yes, obviously that. But also, you as Claire's date to our ten-year high school reunion," she said, nearly laughing as he grimaced. "She was going to flaunt you as her billionaire fiancé."

He exhaled a heavy, frustrated breath. "Yeah, that ship has sailed . . . and sunk, but she's not accepting that it's really over." He raised a brow. "Is that what you have planned for our weekend? Me accompanying you to the reunion?"

"God no," she replied, then reached out and fondly patted his chest through his jacket. "I have something *really* special in mind for you."

"Okay, I'm definitely intrigued," he said, looking amused. "Just tell me when and where."

Oh, how that one sentence conjured up too many risqué scenarios that she quickly forced out of her mind. "My plans are flexible, except for the weekend of my launch next month for my Curvy Girl Couture line of lingerie. When are you free from a Friday afternoon to Sunday?"

He thought for a moment. "How about next weekend?"

She had nothing planned and nodded. "That works for me."

"Don't I at least get a little hint at what we'll be doing?" he asked, giving her a sexy, persuasive smile.

"It's a surprise," she said, knowing that Derek was thinking it would be something fun. And it would be, for her, at least. "I'll text you the details next week."

She was certain, as a businessman, he preferred control over a situation. Not knowing the particulars ahead of time must have accounted for the tiny lines of frustration creasing his forehead. She bit her bottom lip to hold back a laugh, because he had no idea what was in store for him, and that would work to her advantage.

Yes, she was going to enjoy having Derek as her handyman, pool boy, and all-around laborer at her new house for the entire weekend.

Chapter Four

The *not knowing* was driving Derek nuts, and he'd spent too much of Sunday wondering what the hell Jessica had planned that she was being so secretive. He figured he'd find out soon enough, but still, the whole thing, along with Jessica herself, consumed too much of his brain power.

Especially on Monday morning, when he needed it to focus on what Ben was telling him about his meeting with a struggling streaming platform that Blackout Media was interested in acquiring. The other company, MegaReelz, wanted to negotiate a buyout while they were still solvent. But it was clear to both Derek and Ben that their audience and subscriptions were declining and they definitely needed an infusion of cash, as well as an overhaul of their services. After looking at the numbers involved and brainstorming how their firm could elevate the platform to make it competitive in today's market, they both agreed it would be a solid investment.

They discussed financials, signed contracts and other paperwork, and by noon they were fairly well caught up on business and decided to go to a nearby restaurant for lunch. After they'd placed their orders and their drinks were delivered, Ben glanced across the table at Derek with an interested gleam in his eyes.

"I was so focused on sharing all the details of this weekend's meeting with MegaReelz that I forgot all about asking you what happened at the bachelor auction."

"That's fine," Derek said, unwrapping his straw and adding it to his soda.

As soon as he'd stepped into the office that morning, Ben wanted to discuss the possible new venture, which Derek had expected. And once they sat down in the conference room to talk about the pros and cons, both of them had been preoccupied with all the details that came with acquiring a new company.

"Sorry I couldn't be there," Ben said, not sounding apologetic at all but rather more relieved that he'd had a legitimate excuse not to participate. "But I'm dying to know who won you for a weekend of debauchery."

"Your sister," Derek deadpanned.

The smirk on Ben's face turned into an annoyed scowl. "Don't be a dick."

Derek laughed. "I'm not joking."

Ben stared at him, then narrowed his gaze. "Why would she bid on *you*, of all people?"

"My good looks and charm?"

His friend did not look amused. "Seriously. Why would Jessica want to spend a weekend with you and pay for it?"

From Ben's standpoint, Derek understood why the whole situation seemed odd. Women usually bought men at bachelor auctions with some kind of romantic notion in mind, and despite his attraction to Jessica—which he was pretty certain was reciprocated—he didn't get the impression she was going to whisk him away for a seductive rendezvous.

When she said that she had something

really special in mind for him, as much as he'd like to think she meant a weekend of debauchery, there had been something playful about her comment that led him to believe that any kind of seduction wasn't part of her plan.

As it should be, he reminded himself.

"Actually, she did me a huge favor," Derek said as their waitress set their burgers and fries in front of each of them, and once she was gone, he continued. "Claire was at the event, and she was intent on winning me, and for some reason, Jessica must have sensed my dread, and the two of them got into a bidding war."

Ben dragged a French fry through his ketchup. "Considering the rumors that are floating around about Claire's parents being stretched thin financially, which makes sense after what she did to you, could she really afford to spend money so frivolously on a bachelor auction?"

"Probably not," Derek agreed, thinking of the debt she'd racked up on his American Express Black Card behind his back and the pathetic excuses she'd given him. "But clearly that wouldn't stop Claire from doing whatever it took to get what she wanted. It was actually kind of strange, watching the two of them go back and forth, topping each other's bid until Claire finally folded and Jessica won."

"Yeah, how so?" Ben asked before taking a bite of his burger.

"I don't know . . . it's like they had some kind of rivalry going on," he said, thinking back on the whole situation. "I know they went to school together, but they're not really friends or I would have known that during my time with Claire. I mean, at one point, Claire glared at Jessica."

Protective older brother that he was, Ben's lips pursed in annoyance. "Sorry, man, but your ex is a bitch."

"I'm not going to argue the truth." He sighed.

Derek hated that Claire had kept that catty, spiteful part of herself hidden while they'd been dating, but once he'd broken up with her, she'd shown her true colors. He also hated that he'd allowed his own mother to manipulate him and the entire situation.

"I'm sure bidding on me was Claire's way to persuade me to give her another chance, but honestly, I'm just grateful to Jessica for saving me from having to spend an entire weekend with my ex."

Ben's gaze narrowed intently. "You're not really going to have a wild weekend with my sister, right?"

Derek shrugged and smirked, goading his friend. "Hey, it's her call. She won me fair and square."

"Like I said, don't be a dick." Ben took a drink of his soda. "What does she have planned for the two of you?"

"I don't know yet," he said, wiping his greasy fingers on his napkin. "She's going to text me the details this week."

They finished their lunch and headed back to the office. Finally, on Thursday afternoon, Derek received the much-anticipated text message from Jessica, instructing him to bring an overnight bag since he'd be staying at her place, then letting him know what his weekend with her would entail.

Actually, it was a list of things she wanted him to do around the residence she'd just bought outside of the city. Painting the trim on her house. Cleaning the pool. Repairing a section of her wooden fence. Cleaning up the leaves in the yard, mowing the lawn, and tidying up the overgrown hedges. He continued to read. Power wash the driveway and backyard deck. Plant azaleas along the side of the house. Hang outdoor string lights across her back patio.

He frowned at the chores she'd given him. This was what she considered *special*? Okay, so it wasn't the weekend he'd envisioned with Jessica—and really, he had no business envisioning anything at all—but he'd get every last thing on the list accomplished.

He owed her that much.

By Friday afternoon of that week, Jessica was exhausted but exhilarated by everything she'd accomplished over the past five days. She'd finished approving the final details of the Curvy Girl Couture Lingerie launch party with Jade Dare and her assistant, Lauren, over the phone, since the event would be held in one of the smaller ballrooms at the Meridian Hotel.

The food, the drinks, and the décor were set. Entertainment had been booked. Exclusive invitations had been sent out to close friends, key people in the industry, and social media influencers she knew would build hype for the new line of lingerie specifically designed for women with fuller figures.

The photo shoot for the glossy catalog that would be provided at the launch, as well as sent to customers on their mailing list, had gone exceptionally well. The voluptuous models all looked gorgeous in the array of lacy undergarments, flirtatious negligees, satiny loungewear, and provocative boudoir attire. Jessica was confident that she'd have a plethora of amazing, flattering shots to choose from once they were retouched for the final presentation.

Excitement and nerves tumbled in Jessica's stomach as she thought about the golden carrot dangling in front of her and how close she was to grabbing it. It wasn't just the opportunity to provide a luxury line of women's intimate apparel to females who wanted to feel sexy and desirable, but she was in talks with a major retail brand, Belle Demoiselle, who was interested in carrying exclusive-to-them designs of her product in their flagship stores. It was a huge opportunity to expand her reach and gain massive exposure, and she was hoping that the success of the launch would seal the deal.

She'd like to think that kind of an accomplishment would make her mother proud, as well, or even impress her a bit. But Jessica knew not to pin her hopes on that kind of illusion. She'd learned from a very early age that pleasing Amelia Cavanaugh meant being molded into someone and something she wasn't. And anything that had to do with Curvy Girl Couture and embracing the woman she was, was only met with disappointment and criticism. Of course, her mother's constant judgment hurt, but it didn't and wouldn't stop Jessica from pursuing what she loved.

It was after four by the time Jessica finished everything important so she'd have the weekend free to spend with Derek. She was looking forward to watching him work his ass off around her place while she enjoyed making him sweat. Literally. He'd texted her a few hours ago to let her know he was headed to her house to get started on the list she'd sent to him, since most everything that needed to be tended to was outside.

Jessica tidied up the back office desk at

Curvy Girl Couture and made sure she slipped the file folders of information for the launch and brochure into her pale pink attaché case, along with the current design sketches she was drafting just in case she had time in the evenings to work on them. She loved the creative process and found it a relaxing way to unwind before bed.

She walked into the boutique area just as Avery was finishing up with one of their regular customers, who'd purchased a chic faded denim jacket, matching boyfriend jeans, and a flattering pintuck blouse. Avery talked her into adding a cute set of bangle bracelets that would complement the outfit, then bagged up all the items.

"I'm going to head out for the weekend," Jessica said to Avery once the woman was gone and the place was quiet except for Maddie, one of their friends and also a salesgirl at Curvy Girl, who was dressing a mannequin in one of the new sweater dresses that had just come in for the upcoming fall season. "I'll see you and Maddie tomorrow evening, around six, as planned?"

"I personally wouldn't miss it for anything,"

Avery said with a grin. "And Maddie is looking forward to a fun girls' night out, too, aren't you, Maddie?"

"Most definitely!" She draped a chain belt around the mannequin's midsection to show a potential customer how they could accentuate their own curves. "I love that we'll have our own designated driver so we can all enjoy a few drinks while dancing and not have to worry about how we'll get home."

"Does Derek know that he's going to be our personal chauffer to Club Ten29?" Avery asked.

"Not yet. But I'm sure he'll appreciate the break from all the manual labor around my place. Speaking of which . . ."

Jessica dug her cell phone out of her purse and unlocked the screen, intending to take a peek at his progress and possibly get a glimpse of the glistening sweat on his tanned muscles. She could only hope he was working shirtless.

"Let's take a look at how much he's accomplished. I'm not going to lie. Knowing he's getting down and dirty kind of makes me happy —and no innuendos from you, please." She gave Avery a pointed look.

Avery wrinkled her nose at Jessica. "You're no fun."

She tapped on the icon for her indoor/outdoor home security system and opened the one displaying her backyard, where she expected to find Derek, since that's where the majority of work needed to be done.

"I didn't say I wasn't going to enjoy the view, but yeah, for a businessman who is probably used to snapping his fingers and having other people jump to do his bidding, it's going to be very gratifying seeing him out of his designer suits and getting all sweaty and dirty. It will give me a bit of satisfaction for that summer I was grounded because of him . . ."

Her voice trailed off as she stared at the live feed, at first confused as she watched at least half a dozen men she didn't recognize walking around the outside of her house with ladders, power tools, and lawn equipment. Then annoyance quickly followed as she realized what they were doing . . . all the things on her list meant for Derek to complete.

"What. The. Hell?"

Avery moved in close beside her to see the feed on Jessica's phone while she searched the area for the man himself. One of the security cameras found him and her brother relaxing on lounge chairs in the shade by the pool—Derek wearing shorts and a casual shirt, while Ben looked as though he'd come directly from the office in his slacks and white dress shirt. They were each drinking a beer and chatting while watching over the buzz of activity around them, which only made her more irritated.

Avery laughed, which did not improve Jessica's mood. "Yeah, uh, I think he kind of misunderstood the point of you giving him that list."

"You think?" Jessica glared at the images on her phone screen—mainly, at her brother and Derek, who looked like they were on a relaxing vacation. "Why are men so damn obtuse?"

"Because, well, they're men, and being dense when it comes to what goes on in the female mind is part of the territory."

Jessica couldn't argue Avery's logic. "Well, then I guess I need to enlighten him, don't I?"

Chapter Five

Everything was going as planned. Better than planned, actually, Derek thought as he checked to make sure things were getting done the right way.

While the various contractors Derek had hired to complete the tasks on the list Jessica had given him bustled around her small house —more like a cottage, really—he did his best to tune them out while going through his work emails on his laptop. Nothing important or critical—just things that he needed to address that didn't require much concentration.

All the noise was distracting as hell, but he couldn't wait for Jessica to get home and see how much had already gotten done. She was going to be thrilled with all the progress, and he could already imagine her delighted smile and her gratitude for his assistance in contacting the companies and organizing the work. At this rate, everything would probably be finished by tomorrow, well ahead of their three-day time frame.

He glanced up from his laptop as a guy pounded a nail into the board he was securing to the new fence post and caught sight of Ben rounding the side of the house. He strolled over to where Derek was sitting on a lounge chair, his best friend's expression amused as he took in the activity going on around him. From the look of things, Ben came bearing gifts, a six-pack of Coronas in hand.

"Hey, what brings you by?" Derek asked when Ben was close enough to hear him over the noise, surprised to see him there.

The corner of Ben's mouth twitched with a wry smile as he sat down on the lounge chair next to Derek's and set the six-pack on the small table between them. "I thought you might be thirsty and could use a cold beer from all the hard work you've been doing all afternoon in the sun, but clearly, I was wrong."

"You're not wrong," Derek said, grinning as he closed his laptop and set it aside. "A cold beer sounds fantastic. It's warm out today."

They both grabbed a bottle and twisted off the caps. After a few long drinks, Ben's gaze wandered from the landscapers and painters and other workers back to Derek. "I have to say, this isn't what I expected to find when I got here today." He gestured toward the laborers with his free hand.

"Impressive, right?" Derek asked, not giving a shit if he sounded proud of himself for orchestrating so many different crews in such a short amount of time. "I'm going to knock out everything on Jessica's list in no time at all."

Ben tapped his fingers against the side of his bottle of beer. "Uh, yeah . . . I don't think hiring all these contractors to do the work is what my sister had in mind."

"Of course it is," he scoffed, wondering why Ben was being so ridiculous. "You saw the huge list of things she wanted to get done around here."

Ben gave him a speculative look, then finally said, "You know why she's doing this, right? Why she gave you a list of 'chores'?"

He found *chores* an odd word choice. "Yeah, I owe her for bidding on me at the bachelor auction and saving me from ending up with Claire for an excruciating weekend at her high school reunion."

Ben slowly shook his head. "No . . . you owe her from a long time ago."

His friend was confusing the hell out of him. "What are you talking about?"

"You know, it's not my place to say," he replied cryptically. "And if it's an issue, then it's going to be up to Jessica to set you straight."

Derek had a feeling he was missing something important, but since Ben refused to elaborate, Derek didn't press the issue. Instead, he said, "Trust me, she's going to be thrilled."

Except when Jessica showed up half an hour later, she looked anything but delighted with his ingenuity. She walked out of the house to the backyard, using the cemented pathway to make her way to where he and Ben were sitting by the pool, completely ignoring the hustle and bustle of activity going on around her—though it didn't escape Derek's notice that a few of the workers stopped what they were doing to crane their necks and openly eyed her backside as she strode determinedly toward him and Ben.

Even though he was annoyed at their blatant interest, Derek couldn't blame the guys for staring at the way her hips swayed in the fitted black skirt she wore, and he couldn't deny she had fantastic legs, especially in those sexy-as-hell heels currently clicking purposefully against the pavement.

She looked like a woman on a mission, with her chin tipped up and her shoulders pulled back confidently, which only served to draw his gaze to the way her sweater top accentuated her enticing breasts. As she neared, he saw something fiery flash in her eyes, and that bold, fearless glimpse of indignation both confused him and turned him on, because he could only imagine all the ways that kind of passion might play out in the bedroom. . .

Don't say or do something stupid, he silently chastised himself. *Her brother is sitting right next to you and close enough to punch you in your dick for your inappropriate thoughts.*

When she finally reached them, there was no happy smile on her lips. Just an annoyed glare, directed right at him.

"What is all this?" she demanded, waving a hand randomly toward her house.

He honestly had no idea what had her so riled up. "Contractors to do the work you wanted done around your new place?" he said, stating the obvious.

"That's not why I gave you the list," she said, jamming her hands on her hips. "I could have called the damn contractors myself. I didn't need you to do that for me."

He shook his head, his own frustration rising. "Then why—"

"Having paid contractors do the work defeats the purpose of me winning you at the auction," she said, cutting him off. "This was supposed to be payback, not sitting on your ass, delegating tasks while hanging out at the pool and drinking a beer with my brother."

"Payback," he repeated like an idiot, his mind still trying to grasp where he'd gone wrong.

"Yes, *payback*," she said on a low, husky

growl, as if that explained everything, when in fact it left him more bewildered than ever.

"See, I told ya," Ben muttered beneath his breath beside him.

"Send the contractors home, Derek," she said, suddenly looking deflated . . . and dare he say hurt. "I don't want them here, but make sure you pay them double time for inconveniencing them for something you should have done yourself."

She spun around and marched back toward the house, her silky blond waves bouncing down her back and her sassy, curvy ass twitching beneath the formfitting fabric of her skirt.

In a moment of clarity, it finally fucking dawned on him why she was so ticked off. "Aww, shit," he groaned, scrubbing a hand along his jaw. "She expected *me* to do all this work, didn't she?" he said to Ben, even though he still didn't fully understand the payback comment, though he intended to find out.

"Ding, ding, ding," Ben drawled humorously as he put his hand in the air to ring an invisible bell. "Give the man a prize!"

* * *

After sending all the work crews home and making sure they billed him double their rate to make up for cutting their workload short, Derek headed into Jessica's house from the back deck. He found her in the kitchen, standing at the large, marble island, pouring herself a glass of white wine, her back to him. He'd made enough noise entering that she knew he was there, but she didn't turn around.

"Hey," he said, trying to gauge her mood, though he did notice that her stiff posture had softened, almost as if she were defeated. "Can we talk?"

She set the bottle down and turned around, the fire he'd seen outside no longer blazing in her pretty eyes. "Me first. Because I owe you an apology for overreacting," she said with a sigh. "I just didn't want this weekend to be easy on you or something your money could buy, like hiring contractors to do all the work on my to-do list."

He wasn't going to defend himself or his decisions, because he felt like something bigger

61

was at play, and he wanted to understand why Jessica had been so upset.

"I really feel like I'm missing something here." He rubbed his fingers across his forehead. "You said this was supposed to be payback . . . for what?"

"Ugh," she uttered, shaking her head and covering her face with her hands, as if embarrassed. "Now it all seems so foolish and stupid."

He came around the island that was separating them, and when he stood in front of her, he pulled her hands away. "Look at me, Jessica," he said, and when she lifted her pained gaze to his, it took extreme effort not to pull her completely into his arms to alleviate whatever was troubling her. "Clearly, it's not something foolish or stupid to *you*, and I'm not letting it go until you explain."

He brushed his thumbs along the soft skin of her inner wrists before reluctantly releasing her hands. He pulled out a stool from the counter and pointed to it. "Sit," he ordered, and when she was seated, he settled into the stool next to hers, facing her.

She sat primly with her legs together, her hands folded in her lap, while he did the man-spread thing so that his knees bracketed hers. It was meant to make sure she couldn't easily leave, but sitting this close, in such an intimate way, only amped up his awareness of her as a beautiful and, yes, sensual woman.

Growing up with Ben as his best friend, and with four years separating him and Jessica in age, Derek admitted that he'd never seen her in that way, even during her flourishing teenage years. She'd never been on his radar—not during high school, and when college girls had flocked to him, yeah, he'd had his selection of casual sexual encounters. Of course, he'd picked the ones with the best tits and ass, because why not? Intellect, or even her personality, hadn't figured into the equation when it came to getting laid back then. He hadn't been thinking with his brain but his dick, and it reflected in his choice of bed partner.

Now, being older, wiser, and more discriminating—especially after his unpleasant relationship with Claire—he found himself seeing Jessica in a whole new light. As a woman, he'd always found her tempting, and honestly, there was just something about a female with real curves that appealed to him as a grown man who only saw that as part of a whole package. Add in a smart, sassy, confident woman comfortable in her own skin and being true to herself, and yeah, the word *sensual* applied on every level and made his attraction to her that much stronger.

And he wasn't quite sure what to do with that revelation.

He exhaled a deep breath and forced himself to focus on the discussion at hand. "Now, from the beginning. What payback are you referring to?"

Her face flushed, but she didn't avoid the question this time. "Do you remember the summer before my senior year in high school? When Avery and I snuck out to a party and overindulged, and I called you to pick us up because I didn't want my parents or Ben to find out?"

He chuckled. "As if I could forget. The two of you were wasted."

"The first time, for both of us," she admitted with an adorably impish smile. "Avery and I were always outcasts at school, so getting invited was like we finally cracked the cool-kid code or something. But actually, the party sucked, because we both felt this pressure to drink and smoke weed to fit in, and let's face it, Avery and I were not party girls. It was incredibly awkward, and some of the other more popular girls there tried to embarrass us around the guys, making fun of us and the way we . . . looked."

He frowned. "What was wrong with the way you looked?"

She picked up her glass of wine and took a long drink before answering. "We were the fat chicks; therefore, they didn't want us in their little clique or getting friendly with the boys they liked, so they were cruel and callous and did their best to ostracize us."

Learning she'd had to endure that kind of treatment made his jaw clench in anger. As a mature adult, there was no hint of insecurity in Jessica's voice or expression, just a vulnerability that made her human. "Meanness is a mask for insecurity and is usually a form of narcissistic behavior. It's a way for a person to feel superior over someone else, and it's a shitty thing to do."

A small smile tipped up her lips. "And you know this how?"

"I've seen it." For one, Claire had been a

prime example once she'd dropped all pretenses and showed him a glimpse of her true nature and personality. And another . . . "I know Nikki dealt with that a lot during her modeling career, other girls being catty and cruel. Those nude pictures of her that were recently leaked? It was a competitor who wanted to destroy Nikki's career so she'd be the one to take her place in magazine shoots and fashion shows. Didn't end up that way, though. Instead, they found out who was responsible for the photos and it ended up costing the girl *her* career."

"Ahh, poetic justice. I love it," Jessica said, raising her wineglass in a mock toast before finishing off the rest of her drink.

"So, back to your story," he encouraged, not wanting her to get distracted.

She nodded, licked the remnants of wine from her lips—which he had the urge to do himself—and set her empty glass back down on the island. "Remember how I swore you to secrecy about Avery and me sneaking out to the party and getting drunk and stoned? Well, a few days later, my mother overheard you telling Ben the story."

She arched an accusing brow, and he grimaced. "My bad," he muttered, still feeling a tad guilty about that. "I was just being protective and wanted to make sure that Ben kept an eye on you so you didn't do it again."

She rolled her eyes. "I had one older, protective brother, and I didn't need another. And as a result of your big mouth, my mother ended up grounding me for the rest of the summer."

He winced. "Yeah, I remember your brother mentioning that."

"And the worst part?" she went on. "My mother deliberately made sure I was grounded during the two weeks I was supposed to go with Avery and her family to their lake house. My mother knew how much I'd been looking forward to that vacation. It was like my one escape, and I loved being with Avery's family because they are so kind and accepting and treated me like their own daughter. And instead, I was stuck at home with a list of chores to do every single day as punishment. I honestly think my mother was hoping that all the sweating would help slim me down."

"What?" He was certain he'd heard that last comment wrong.

She shrugged indifferently, but there was a pained look in her eyes he didn't miss. "My mother wasn't exactly happy with my weight issues, either. She found it embarrassing that she had a chubby daughter, and I was always made to feel that I was just never good enough because of it, even though I'd been diagnosed with PCOS and that was a known symptom."

"PCOS?" he asked, confused, since he'd never heard the term before.

"Polycystic ovary syndrome," she explained. "It's a female thing. There are issues with hormonal imbalances and a woman's metabolism, which can make it difficult to lose weight and keep it off."

Jesus, her mother was a piece of work . . . just like his own was, and he hated that she'd had to endure that kind of criticism. Probably still did.

"So, anyway," she said, bringing the conversation back around to their original topic. "I might have saved you from spending a weekend with Claire at the bachelor auction, but I'll admit that I was looking forward to payback for that summer of being grounded because you blabbed to my brother. You owe me for that."

He chuckled. "Okay, I get it." And *now*, he really did.

An idea came to him, and without thinking, he leaned forward and placed his hands on her knees, his fingers caressing the soft, bare skin there. "I know a lot of the items on the list are nearly finished, but what I missed doing in hard labor, how about I make up for in other ways?"

Her lashes fell half-mast, and a sultry smile curved her lips. "Other ways?" she asked in an intrigued tone.

He nodded, then stood up, refilling her wineglass before helping her to her feet. With one hand clasping hers and the other holding her drink, he asked, "Which way to your bedroom?"

Her eyes widened, not in shock but in a way he found much too tempting. Like she was thinking dirty thoughts, about them, together, in said bedroom. And God help him, he wasn't opposed to the idea, despite knowing it was a line he shouldn't ever consider crossing.

Her tongue skimmed across her full bottom

lip and he blatantly watched it. "My, uh, bedroom?" she repeated. "Why?"

His grin was deliberately slow and sexy, his words equally seductive. "Because I think you need to relax, and I have just the thing in mind."

Chapter Six

With every inch of her body hyperaware of Derek leading her upstairs to her bedroom, his big, warm hand engulfing her smaller one, Jessica's mind ran wild with all the various ways this gorgeous, hot man could make her relax.

Maybe a back massage to ease the tension in her muscles? Or an orgasm or two to alleviate her stress? Or what if his idea of a payback included hot, toe-curling sex? Mmm, she wasn't opposed to the idea, and the thought almost made her moan out loud. It had been way too long since she'd been pleasured with anything or anyone besides her battery-operated boyfriend, and the image of indulging with Derek, the one man who made her entire body hum with desire, had her stomach flipping with anticipation.

Why else would he be taking her to her bedroom?

"I assume you have a connecting bathroom and a tub?" he asked as he followed her directions down the short hall until he reached the double doors leading into the primary bedroom.

"Yes," she replied.

She'd fallen in love with the porcelain claw-foot tub the previous owners had installed during a renovation, especially since it was big enough for two, not that she'd ever shared it with anyone. But taking a long, luxurious bath was one of her favorite indulgences.

Once inside the bedroom, he walked her over to the queen-sized bed and made her sit down. He put her glass of wine on the dresser, then knelt in front of her and slipped off the heels she'd worn all day. Her breath caught in surprise, then coalesced into a sigh of contentment as he rubbed the ball of her foot and instep, then massaged her calves like an expert masseuse.

Her eyes rolled back with the pleasure of it.

God, his hands were like magic, and she suddenly wanted them to travel much, much higher.

"Are you starting to forgive me for hiring all those contractors?" he asked, a knowing smirk on his face.

She laughed lightly, then moaned as his fingers dug gently into the taut muscles along her calves. "Maybe a little," she conceded.

"Maybe, if I stayed right here on my knees and tried another tactic, I might fully convince you of how sorry I really am?"

He was teasing, being the flirtatious Derek she knew that came so naturally to him, and she found herself being just as playful, because why not? She'd had one glass of wine—on an empty stomach, no less—and it made her bolder than normal. "Depends on what that tactic might be."

He arched a wicked brow. "I'm open to suggestions," he murmured, as if leaving those ideas up to her.

His fingers stroked behind the back of her knee—that sensitive erogenous zone that made her sex clench and nipples tighten into aching peaks—and she swallowed hard and shivered. "Derek . . ." Her voice trailed off breathlessly.

Suddenly, he swore beneath his breath and his hands dropped away. Abruptly, he stood. "Stay here and give me a minute."

He quickly turned around but unless her eyes were deceiving her—and she was positive they weren't—there was a telltale bulge in his shorts. As in, whatever that moment had been between them, he'd been caught up in the sexual tension, too.

He needed a minute, and honestly, so did she, because *what the hell was that?* She'd been attracted to Derek for what seemed like forever, but he'd always treated her like a sister, undoubtedly out of respect for Ben being his best friend and, now, his business partner. Sure, there'd been a level of teasing between them, but never had things gotten that intense. Up until now, she would have bet every penny in her trust fund that he didn't see her as a sexy, desirable woman.

But in that moment, she'd felt both of those things, and his unexpected reaction to their interaction confused the hell out of her.

Maybe it was just a fluke, because she knew

she wasn't the type of woman Derek normally dated. Yeah, that had to be it. A total fluke.

She watched him head into the adjoining en suite. "What are you doing?" she asked curiously.

"Drawing you a bath," he said, plugging the drain and turning on the faucets to full blast.

From her seated position on the bed, she could see the tub and the main part of the bathroom, as well as Derek as he surveyed the area. He looked at the bottles lined up on a shelf near the tub, where she kept an assortment of bubble bath, body oils, and bath bombs. He unscrewed the top of one of the pretty, jewel-encrusted glass vials she collected and sniffed the contents. That scent, she knew, was gardenias, and he must have liked the fragrance because he added a small pour to the cascade of running water. He grabbed one of her large, fluffy towels and draped it over the heated rack, then turned it on so she'd have a nice warm towel to wrap herself in after her bath.

He was a man in charge, and it was super hot to watch him take control.

On the small side table at the head of the tub were a few other items. A book she'd been reading. A scented candle that Derek lit. And a vintage iPod she'd kept from her high school days that still held some of her favorite songs. He picked up the device, turned it on, and selected a mellow Colbie Caillat song.

He added her glass of wine to the side table, then dimmed the raindrop chandelier overhead so the bathroom was mostly lit by candlelight. When the tub was three-quarters full, he finally turned off the water, a fragrant steam billowing from the surface.

"Okay, come on in," he finally invited, and when she stepped inside, he gave her a mock bow. "Derek Bettencourt, at your service, for the rest of the weekend."

She laughed at his playful demeanor. "I'm impressed. Looks like you've done this a time or two," she teased.

"Actually, never," he admitted, surprising her. "But it's not hard to figure out how to run water into a tub or see the things you enjoy while taking a bath."

Regardless, she found the gesture incredibly thoughtful. "This is . . . nice. Thank you."

He gave her a genuine smile. "You deserve

to be indulged, and I hope this helps make up for my earlier faux pas."

"It's definitely a start."

He chuckled. "Good to know I can redeem the situation and myself. Now, while you're relaxing, I'm going to go take care of dinner . . . unless you need me to stick around to scrub your back?"

That flirtatious gleam was back in his eyes, and as much as she wanted to see what he'd do if she said yes, she shook her head. "Thank you, but that's what that loofah with the long handle is for," she said, pointing toward the back scrubber hanging from a peg beneath the shelf with her body oils and other bath items.

"Don't say I didn't offer," he said, and with a shameless wink, he left her alone in the bathroom, closing the door after him.

Anxious to enjoy her bath and the relaxing ambiance, she stripped out of her clothes and clipped her hair into a messy bun on top of her head, then sank into the gloriously hot, gardenia-scented water up to her shoulders.

She leaned her head back against the small pillow suctioned onto the lip of the porcelain tub and closed her eyes, a content sigh escaping her lips as she felt her entire body go lax.

She'd taken probably a hundred or more baths over the years, but none that someone else had prepared for her. It was a nice, luxurious feeling to be spoiled and pampered, even in this simplistic way. Not even her previous, long-term boyfriend had done something so sweet and considerate for her.

Then again, she'd quickly learned that Noah—an accountant at her father's investment firm—didn't have a romantic bone in his body. He'd always been practical, realistic, and efficient. And precise, especially when it came to how well ordered and planned out his life was. She'd been naively okay with those personality quirks . . . until they began affecting her directly.

His emotional manipulation started out in subtle ways . . . his opinions on what to wear that *he* found more flattering and appropriate, especially around his co-workers and business associates. Criticism about the meals she ate and how the ratio of carbs to vegetables was unbalanced—*and did she really need that dessert?* How her long, wavy hair wasn't suited for the kind of refined, sophisticated woman he needed by his side. Recommendations of ways to lose weight, and when she didn't conform to any of his suggestions, disagreements turned to arguments and, eventually, harsh ultimatums that had backfired on Noah.

He'd thought he could control her life and mold her into his ideal of a perfect girlfriend and eventually wife. He'd mistakenly believed that her life revolved around him. He'd been so certain she'd be willing to completely change herself, physically and mentally, to please him —though she doubted he'd ever be truly happy with her, despite any changes she made—and he'd been shocked when *she'd* rejected his final demands with a very unladylike *fuck you, I'm not changing for any man*, then walked out on him.

But despite her bravado, she couldn't deny how much it hurt that she hadn't been good enough just the way she was. It hadn't helped when her pissed-off mother informed Jessica that she'd allowed *such a great catch* to get away, and she'd probably never find another man like Noah.

If that were the case, then Jessica didn't

want another man. Especially not one like Noah.

Refusing to let those memories ruin Derek's sweet gesture, she took a drink of her wine and let herself fully enjoy the bath, the candlelight, and the soothing music. With her head cushioned on the pillow and her body warm and relaxed, she drifted off into a nap. When she awoke, she knew by the song that was playing, one by a different artist, that about half an hour had passed. The water was also lukewarm, and when she lifted her hands, her fingers were pruned.

She had no idea what Derek was making for dinner, but she didn't want to keep him waiting, so she stepped out of the tub, then used the heated towel to dry off her skin—now soft and silky and fragrant from the oil he'd put in the water.

She left her hair up and changed into her favorite loungewear for the evening—a soft, cotton, long-sleeved top with a loose neckline and comfortable drawstring pants—then headed downstairs. She inhaled the scent of something rich and savory, and her stomach grumbled loudly.

When she entered the kitchen, she expected to see pots and pans on the stove, ingredients cluttering the counters, and unwashed dishes in the sink, but her kitchen was spotless, except for the delivery bags on the island with the name of the restaurant they came from: Nonna Vittoria, an authentic, family-owned and operated Italian restaurant.

She glanced over to the kitchen table, where Derek was pouring them each a glass of red wine.

"You cheated," she accused playfully.

"Trust me," he drawled as his gaze slowly flickered down, then back up her body. "I figured it was more important to feed you something edible than make you suffer with my awful cooking." He pulled out a chair and gestured for her to sit.

She slid into the chair and grinned at him as he settled into the seat next to hers. "Not much of a chef, huh?"

"Not one of my finer talents." He grinned wickedly, leaving her to wonder about those other superior talents. "I mean, I can do the basics, but no one does chicken marsala like

Nonna Vittoria, so why even try and compete with that?"

"Good point," she agreed.

As he plated her food, and she took a moment to appreciate the chicken breast smothered in mushrooms that had been sauteed in marsala wine and cream sauce. It looked and smelled delicious. "I love that you ordered something rustic and authentic, instead of from one of those fancy fusion places that are popping up all over the city."

"I'm a traditional guy. I like my food authentic." He smiled and raised his wineglass toward her, and she did the same, clicking the rim to his in a toast. "Enjoy, but make sure you save room for dessert."

"I always save room for dessert," she said, pleased that he hadn't skimped on that part of the meal.

They ate quietly for a few minutes, and she thought back to the auction and how panicked he'd looked when Claire bid on him. Jessica was still curious about his reaction. Besides, she'd always found it difficult to reconcile his relationship and engagement to Claire in her mind.

She never would have paired them as a couple. Derek was kind and thoughtful and caring—she'd seen those traits in the way he treated his sister, Nikki. Claire was . . . all about herself. Selfish, pretentious, and disingenuous. The match, from the beginning, had struck Jessica as unexpected. Sure, there was that saying that opposites attract, but not to those kinds of extremes.

"So . . . do you mind if I ask you a personal question, about Claire?"

He stiffened ever so slightly, then covered it up with a shrug. "Not my favorite topic, but sure. What would you like to know?"

"I know this is probably going to come off as rude, but what did you see in Claire to make you want to date her, then propose to her?"

He huffed out a laugh as he cut a slice of the chicken breast. "Ahh, going right for the jugular, huh?"

She heard the self-deprecation in his voice and quickly gave him a way out. "I'm sorry. You don't have to answer if it makes you uncomfortable."

"No, it's okay." He eyed her speculatively. "I know you went to high school with Claire, but have you known her very well since then?"

Jessica swallowed the bite she'd just taken, trying not to choke on the piece of meat as it went down. "Umm, no." She hadn't told him that Claire had been one of the mean girls at that summer party they'd talked about earlier, or her nemesis in high school. This conversation wasn't about Jessica's relationship with Claire but Derek's, and she didn't want to mix the two. "We didn't and don't run in the same social circles."

"Probably a good thing that you didn't know her well," he said ruefully, right before he took a long drink of his wine, probably for fortitude. "I knew *of* Claire because my parents are friends with her mother and father, and my mother had nothing but wonderful, flattering things to say about her. Actually, her father is one of my father's political donors, and now that I'm able to take a huge step back from the situation and see it more objectively, I know my mother and hers were manipulating me because they were hoping to merge the families."

She wrinkled her nose at him. "Isn't that a bit antiquated?"

He laughed. "Yes. But it still happens between rich and powerful families, and I honestly didn't realize what was going on. At the time, I was wrapped up in negotiations for Blackout Media to purchase a digital platform, so I was just going through the motions with Claire . . . dating her because it was expected, taking her to events as my plus-one, showing up to family events with her on my arm because it was easier than dealing with my mother's twenty questions about my feelings for Claire. I was really more focused on work and expanding our media outlets, and I kind of just fell into the relation-ship, and doing things with Claire just became a habit because it was easy, if that makes sense?"

She ate a few sauteed mushrooms and nodded. "I get it." And she really did, consid-ering her own relationship with Noah. "And what about getting engaged?"

"Pure pressure," he admitted with a sigh as he set his knife and fork down on his plate. "From Claire. My mother and her mother. Hell, even my father, though he didn't often express an opinion. My mother went on about what a great couple we were, that I wasn't getting any younger and I should start thinking about starting a family and how I'd already disappointed my parents by not following my father into politics. My mother is a master manipulator, and I'll admit, she got in my head. Again, it was easier to go through the motions and get engaged than to deal with the constant reminder of what a disappointment I was."

Finished with her own meal, Jessica pushed her plate aside and reached for her wine, taking a drink. "I take it you finally realized the mistake you'd made with Claire?"

"A *mistake* is an understatement," he muttered, leaning back in his chair, the look in his eyes troubled. "The entire time I was dating Claire, she was always on her best behavior. Sweet. Kind. Understanding. I swear, there were no red flags until that ring was on her finger. It's like knowing we were getting married made her more lax and careless about her real attitude. It wasn't long before I started noticing how she treated the waitstaff when we went out to dinner or how rudely she'd talk to people she felt were beneath her. I heard rumors about her saying shitty things about Nikki and her modeling career behind her back." He shook his head in frustration. "Claire's entire demeanor changed, and the more I saw this entitled, spoiled woman emerge, the more I realized that her behavior was too ingrained to be some kind of new personality trait."

Jessica could vouch for who the real Claire was, but she didn't want to sound like a jealous or petty person. "I'm really sorry," she said softly. "I know what it's like not to live up to the standard your parents set. And I'm even more sorry you had to learn the hard way about Claire."

He absently tapped his finger against his empty wineglass. "I think the worst part was, since I wasn't as attentive and present as I should have been in the relationship, Claire totally took advantage of me and the situation."

"How so?" she asked curiously.

"The final catalyst that led to me ending things was when I got a call from my accountant, who wanted to make sure I was aware of the excessive charges on my American Express Black Card, which he handles for me," Derek said, a bitter note tinging his voice. "The charges were from places that I wouldn't normally shop, mostly online luxury designer websites like Chanel, Louis Vuitton, Gucci, Prada, those types of stores. When I finally took a look at the statement, there were over a hundred thousand dollars in charges that I didn't make. Claire did."

Jessica's mouth opened in shock. "Holy crap," she said before she could stop herself.

"Holy crap is right," Derek agreed. "She'd taken my card number at some point, along with all the pertinent information, and went on a fucking shopping spree."

"Did you, umm, confront her?" she asked, hoping she wasn't being too nosey.

"Oh, hell yeah, I did," he said in a fierce tone. "I came right out and asked her about the charges, and she didn't deny them. Instead, she used the excuse that her father had cut back on her spending allowance, and if we were going to be married, she needed to 'look the part,'" he said, using air quotes, "of being a Bettencourt, and she didn't think I would care if she bought 'a few things.'"

Jessica cringed, feeling bad for Derek. "I'll admit, that's a bit ballsy."

"You think?" He shook his head in disgust. "She was actually *offended* that I was angry and she had zero remorse. The thing is, I wouldn't deny my wife or fiancée something she wanted. Hell, I can more than afford it, but the fact that Claire had no problem going behind my back, being so cavalier about taking my credit card information, and racking up massive debt without discussing it with me was what really pissed me off."

Jessica sat in silent disbelief and let Derek get everything off his chest, which he seemed to need to do.

"There've been rumors that her father is having financial issues and her family is living beyond their means, which is probably why he cut back on her spending allowance. Never mind that she should have a job that paid for the things she wanted," he muttered. "But the whole situation, along with her dishonesty and lack of accountability, opened my eyes to just how shallow she is, and I was done because I didn't trust her," he said with a shake of his head.

"I don't blame you," she said.

"I was nothing more than a meal ticket that let her maintain her upscale lifestyle and keep up appearances in the affluent social circles that are important to her but I don't give a shit about." He dragged his fingers through his hair in agitation and exhaled a harsh breath. "*And,* the insane thing is, my mother thinks I should forgive Claire and give her another chance."

Jessica blinked in surprise. "I had no idea about any of that," she said, shifting in her chair in a way that caused the loose, open neckline of her top to slip down one shoulder. Derek eyed her exposed skin, his gaze lingering before he casually reached out and guided the material back in place.

He covered up her shoulder, something she found amusing since it was part of the design. "I'm glad you didn't find out those things *after* you got married."

"The truth is, I was having doubts about Claire before the whole credit card issue. I didn't love her. Those doubts, along with seeing a side she'd never shown me before, were something I couldn't ignore, no matter how much my parents were hoping for a political arrangement."

"Sounds like Claire is hoping for a reconciliation, too," Jessica said, recalling the things she'd overheard the other woman say at the bachelor auction.

He shook his head hard. "Not gonna happen, though it's not like she hasn't tried," he said. "After I ended things, she switched personalities back to sweet Claire and tried calling and texting to say how sorry she was and assuring me that she'd changed." He scoffed. "I think being manipulative is so ingrained that it's impossible for her to change. Remember our narcissist discussion earlier?"

She nodded.

"Claire is a textbook example. No self-awareness or empathy, and everything is all about her." He sighed, the sound heavy and weighted, then met Jessica's gaze with a grimace. "Damn, that was a lot to unload on you."

She smiled at him. "Well, I *did* ask about her."

"The last thing I want to think about right now, or even this weekend, is Claire," he said, his mood shifting easily, leaving all that intensity and frustration behind as he gave her one of his flirtatious grins. "So, how about we move on to something more . . . tempting."

Tempting . . . the word was so filled with possibilities. "Such as?"

"Dessert." He leaned closer, his eyes falling to her lips. "*Chocolate* dessert."

She laughed. "I will never say no to sweets, *especially* if it's chocolate. That's temptation personified."

"Hmm, I'm learning all your vices," he hummed in a tone that sent tremors of awareness tingling along her spine. "So, if I want you to spill your secrets, all I have to do is persuade you with chocolate?"

She nodded, mesmerized by the alluring sound of his voice and the inviting twinkle in his eyes. "Yes, pretty much."

A slow, sinful smile curved his lips. "Good to know."

Oh, man. She was in trouble. The kind she knew she'd enjoy way too much.

Chapter Seven

After that heavy conversation with Jessica about his relationship with Claire, Derek needed a moment to regroup. He took the opportunity to clear the dishes from the table—insisting Jessica not do a thing—and retreated to the kitchen to fetch dessert, a double chocolate mousse cake with caramel drizzle.

As he switched the cake from the Styrofoam container to a regular plate, he realized he could have kept the details of the breakup streamlined. A simple *things just didn't work out between us* would have sufficed, but once he'd started talking, all the sordid details flooded out.

For more than six months, he'd kept everything bottled up inside and hadn't known how much he needed the release. It wasn't as though he could have discussed the emotional and mental turmoil Claire had put him through with his parents, who *still* wanted him to marry the woman. His sister had been going through her own ordeal and he hadn't wanted to burden her. And he'd even glossed over the details with Ben because who the hell really wanted to hear him rant about relationship drama?

But Jessica was easy to talk to, and once he'd started, the words wouldn't stop. It had felt good to get it *all* out there and off his chest. She'd offered no judgment or criticism, just an understanding he'd desperately needed. He couldn't recall the last time he'd been with a woman he trusted and could talk to without couching his words or feelings. Tonight showed him a side of Jessica he hadn't been aware of before, and he wasn't referring to her soft, curvy body and the confidence she'd grown into over the years. A guy would have to be dead not to notice those things. But she'd given him a glimpse beneath the surface to the woman she'd become.

She'd displayed a human vulnerability while talking about the summer she'd been grounded and how badly her mother had treated her, and when listening to him spill his guts, she'd offered him compassion and kindness. Jessica was unassuming and real, without pretense covering up her genuine personality. She was a refreshing change, highlighting how superficial so many of his relationships had become.

Grabbing a fork, he walked back to the dining area with the dessert in hand, determined to keep things light and fun going forward. When he sat down beside her and she saw the cake, Jessica's eyes lit up with delight, and she pouted adorably when he placed the plate in front of himself and not her.

"Don't I get a piece?" she asked, eyes crinkled in confusion.

"This *is* your piece." He slid the fork into the cake, sectioning off a bite, then held it up to her lips.

A startled look passed over her face. "What are you doing?"

"I'm feeding you dessert." He grinned. "I'm at your beck and call for the weekend, remember? And I'm trying to make up for those earlier boneheaded assumptions I made about doing the stuff outside."

"Well, if you insist..." Her lips lifted in a smile. As she leaned forward, the slight movement caused the neckline of her top to slip down her arm again, and he was no longer surprised when his cock reacted to the sight of her creamy skin. He shifted and hoped she didn't notice, but she was too focused on the treat in front of her.

Parting her lips, she let him feed her the mousse cake, moaning as all that chocolatey goodness melted on her tongue. The arousing sound went straight to his dick, and in an attempt to distract himself, he readjusted the collar of her sweatshirt. He slid the material back up to her shoulder, trying not to let his fingers linger on her soft skin.

He continued to feed her bites of cake, and after too many sexy moans of appreciation, she sat back and met his gaze. "I guess now is as good a time as any to tell you that you'll be driving me, Avery, and Maddie to Club Ten29 tomorrow night."

Once again, her top slipped. He readjusted it and her lips quirked in a cute smile.

"So, I'll be chaperoning you, huh?"

She rolled her eyes. "I'm a big girl, Derek," she said, skimming her tongue along her bottom lip to catch a smear of the mousse. "I don't need a chaperone to go dancing. Just someone to drop us off and make sure we get home safely after a few drinks. Are you good with that?"

Great. Just how he wanted to spend tomorrow night, watching Jessica flirt and dance with other men. His reaction took him off guard. Since when had he cared about what she did?

"Sure. It's fine," he said, lying, as he fed her another morsel. He set the fork on the plate, wondering why he was already annoyed at the prospect of another guy or *guys* ogling or touching Jessica.

And Jesus Christ, it was driving him nuts that the open neckline of her top kept slipping down her arm in a way that was too damn sexy. Once again he pushed it back into place. This time, she shivered as his fingers accidentally grazed the side of her neck and his shorts grew too damned tight.

"You don't need to keep doing that." Her amused smile returned, but her voice was low and husky. "It's just going to happen again."

"Then I'm going to have to readjust it again." He pursed his lips, aware he was being unreasonable.

"Derek, the sweatshirt is meant to be worn off the shoulder," she insisted. "It's okay to leave it the way it is."

"It's dangerous to leave it that way," he said, shocking them both with the low growl of his voice.

She held his gaze, her amusement fading, something more seductive and daring flickering in her eyes. "Why?"

Did he admit the truth or lie and protect them both? That was his dilemma. He decided to be honest and deal with the consequences. "Because the sight makes me want to touch and lick every inch of your soft skin. And not just on your shoulder."

"Oh." Her lips parted, and her eyes widened.

She obviously hadn't expected him to admit he desired her, and he stood up before he did something incredibly stupid. Like haul her into his lap and kiss her senseless. Or pick her up and haul her upstairs to her bedroom, where he'd bury his face between her thighs and make her moan his name. *Fuck.*

"I should clean up the kitchen." Before she could say anything in response, he spun around and left her sitting alone in the dining area.

He exhaled a deep breath as he began throwing the restaurant cartons and bags in the trash, then started to wash the dishes. Just as he was finishing up, he heard the light tinkling of glass and turned around as Jessica entered the room—with the damned neckline draped down one arm, ignoring his previous warning.

He didn't miss the sensual, almost daring look in her eyes, the slight bounce of her breasts, or the sway of her hips as she closed the distance between them. She was holding two empty wineglasses in one hand and the dessert plate in the other and set the drinkware in the sink.

A heap of fluffy mousse remained on the dish and he automatically said, "You still have one bite left."

She tossed the fork into the sink and handed him the plate. "Then feed it to me."

The words came out like a dare since, without the fork, she clearly expected him to use his fingers. Who was this bold, sassy woman, and what had she done with the Jessica he thought he knew?

Was she aware that he was not the type of guy to back down from a challenge? She was about to find out. With his index finger, he swiped the last piece of chocolate mousse on the plate and brought it up to her mouth. "Open up," he ordered.

To his surprise, she did, letting him push his finger and the last bit of dessert into her waiting mouth. With her seductive gaze holding his, she closed her lips around his finger, and instead of pulling it back out like he should have, Derek waited to see what she'd do next.

She didn't disappoint. Her soft tongue curled over the tip, and his brain went straight into the gutter, imagining she was licking his stiff cock instead. The swipe of her tongue might as well have been directly on his already throbbing dick. As she took the length in her mouth and sucked off the sweet, choco-latey mousse with greedy enthusiasm, a soft moan of pleasure echoed from the back of her throat.

It was all he could do not to drop the plate and adjust his straining erection with his free hand. And when she finished, she released him with a pop and licked her bottom lip, as if not wanting to miss a single dollop of chocolate. It was an erotic invitation, and his entire body vibrated with the need to taste her. After setting the plate on the counter, he slid his hand to the side of her neck, wishing for a moment that she'd left her hair down so he had the opportunity to know what those silky strands would feel like tangled around his fingers.

He grazed her jawline with his thumb, then pushed her chin up, raising her mouth, giving her every opportunity to stop the madness. She didn't. Her lashes fell to half-mast, and she waited, unmoving, for him to close the short distance between them.

Fuck it. Done resisting their attraction, he finally kissed her.

At first touch, she gasped, then moaned, her lips parting to let his tongue sweep inside. She tasted sweet, like chocolate, and so addicting he craved *more*. Pressing his body to hers, he backed her up until they hit the counter, and when he had her cornered, he rolled his hips, letting her feel the thick length of his cock straining the front of his shorts. She let out a soft, kittenish mewl and slid her hands up his chest and around his neck, tilting her hips to his, as if trying to fit his erection between her thighs to find some kind of relief.

Their mouths hadn't parted, and God, there was so much hunger in the kiss. So much heat and passion in her response, it lit his blood on fire. Need spiked through him and damnable thoughts flew through his head. Thoughts of spinning her around so she faced the counter. Of shoving her lounge pants and panties down her legs, ditching his shorts, and discovering how warm and tight her pussy would feel wrapped around his aching cock. Or how her lush ass would cushion his hard, driving thrusts as he fucked her from behind.

Knowing he was teetering on the edge of doing something far more reckless than a kiss, he tore his mouth from hers.

She moaned a protest. "Derek," she whispered, and he didn't miss the aching need in her voice.

"I know." He pressed his forehead against hers and groaned, and when their heavy breathing subsided, he lifted his head and framed her face in his hands. "But I shouldn't have touched you. I shouldn't be kissing you. And I damned sure shouldn't be thinking about all the dirty, filthy things I want to do to you," he said, hoping that if he heard the words out loud, he'd convince himself to do the right thing and let her go. Because when he'd slipped his finger between her lips with that chocolate mousse, he hadn't been thinking at all. Not of the consequences or all the reasons he had *not* to give in to temptation.

Until she tried to obliterate his good intentions. "What if I want you to?"

She bit into her lush, kiss-swollen lower lip, and his restraint nearly snapped like a twig. But he didn't react to the longing in her gaze or the lust etching her features. No matter how much he wanted to.

If she was any other woman, Derek wouldn't hesitate to take this encounter to its logical conclusion. But that was the problem.

She wasn't any other woman. She was his best friend and business partner's sister, and he respected Ben too much to cross that line. Not to mention, there was so much at stake if things between him and Jessica went south.

Besides, he'd be a fucking hypocrite to sleep with Jessica when he'd given Asher a heap of shit for sleeping with his own sister, Nikki, on his private island. Derek's issue with Asher had more to do with the age gap than bro-code, but still . . . if Derek fucked Jessica and did something stupid to hurt her, he'd screw up not just his friendship with Ben but their partnership and successful business, as well.

And he just couldn't take that risk.

Jessica took a step back, her action bringing him out of his thoughts. "I guess silence does speak volumes. I suppose that kiss was you fulfilling your duty? Making sure I got some-thing for the money I spent buying you for the weekend?"

"*What?*" It took him a minute to process what she meant. It was the obstinate tilt of her chin and the flicker of self-doubt in her gaze that made him understand. "You think I kissed you out of obligation because you won my services for the weekend? That what just happened between us was a *pretense* on my part?"

She shrugged and crossed her arms over her chest, the movement clearly self-protective. "Why else would you stop?"

Jesus. He hated himself for causing her to doubt him. "Because there's more involved here than just me and you," he said, making sure she knew his decision had nothing to do with her personally.

"I don't understand," she said, her hands still wrapped tightly around herself.

He ran his fingers through his hair. "It's ... I can't risk the possibility of putting a strain on my working relationship with Ben. Trust me, if my dick had a vote, we'd be up in your bedroom and you'd already be naked beneath me. But I'm trying to be smart and not do something either of us might regret."

She shook her head and sighed, her arms dropping to her sides, her lips puckered in an adorable frown. "I guess I understand . . ." she said, the glint back in her eyes, and he felt so much fucking better. Still hard and aroused.

But glad she wasn't hurting. "But just so you know, I wouldn't regret anything."

Fuck me. That mischievous sparkle in her gaze should have warned him. With a groan, he pointed to the doorway leading to the living room. "*Go,*" he ordered in a low, playful growl. "Before I do something even more drastic."

She didn't move, purposely defying him. "Like what?" she asked, her tone back to sassy and sexy.

He had the distinct impression she wasn't going to let this kiss go. He'd opened Pandora's box and there was no going back. No matter what valid protests he had. She'd never want to jeopardize his friendship or business with her brother, but this new-to-him Jessica obviously had her own agenda. His only choice was to freak her out enough that she'd be the one backing away.

He took a warning step toward her. "Like putting you over my knee and spanking your ass for thinking I'd pretend *anything* with you."

Her lips parted, but instead of a horrified gasp, her eyes darkened and her cheeks flushed a healthy shade of red. But she didn't make a move to leave. She also didn't push the issue any further. So Derek did the only thing he could and walked out of the kitchen first.

A man only had so much willpower, and Jessica Cavanaugh was clearly going to test every ounce he possessed.

Chapter Eight

Unable to sleep, Jessica put on a silky robe over her short nightgown, tied the sash around her waist, then left her bedroom. No light showed beneath the closed door of the guest room across the hallway, where Derek was sleeping. Clearly, he didn't seem to have any issues dozing off tonight.

It was after midnight, but it wasn't unusual for design ideas to keep her awake until she got up to put them on paper. She'd learned the hard way that if she didn't jot down notes or sketches immediately, even if she swore she'd remember everything in the morning, she rarely did. And losing an idea like the one in her head right now would keep her tossing and turning, so it was just easier to get out of bed and follow her muse.

She headed to the kitchen first, to make herself a hot cup of chamomile tea. While she waited for the water in the kettle to boil, then for the tea bag to steep, she couldn't help but remember Derek's hot kiss that had practically melted her panties and had her on the verge of begging for more, and the conversation that transpired afterward. How he'd made it clear that even though he'd ended things before they went too far, his desire for her had been genuine. Knowing their attraction was mutual, at least, helped soothe the doubts and insecurities that had tried to claw their way to the surface.

They'd spent the rest of the evening casually hanging out. Derek suggested they watch a movie on Netflix—he'd selected an action-adventure flick, not a hint of romance or sex in the plot—and he'd sat down in the single recliner while she curled up on the sofa. Clearly, he didn't want to risk any chance of them touching.

She dunked her tea bag a few more times

before squeezing out the excess liquid, still amused by his attempts to keep things platonic. How he'd deliberately maintained a respectable distance. Kept any excess touching to a minimum. And made sure their conversations were light and friendly, without any sexual overtures.

Jessica understood the crux of Derek's concern about her brother and their business partnership. That whole mixing-business-with-pleasure thing came with risks, and as much as she wanted more than one kiss with Derek, she needed to respect his decision. The last thing she'd ever want to do was make things awkward between Ben and Derek.

But that didn't mean she couldn't flirt with him. Drive him a little crazy with a bit of playful teasing. Let the sexual tension between them simmer and burn, just for the fun of it. Because one thing she'd learned, she and Derek had fun together and she'd earned this weekend. Purchased it anyway, she mused. So, yeah, she liked that idea. A lot.

Smiling at the thought, she picked up her cup of tea and went to her office, located down the hall from the kitchen. She flipped on the light, set her cup down on the drafting table, and opened her sketch pad to a clean page.

She always started with a basic concept on paper, and once she was satisfied with the draft, she switched to an illustrator program on her computer, where she could add depth, textures, and finer details, then generate as many iterations of the original design as she wanted.

Beginning with an outline of a curvier, full-figured woman's body as a template, she switched out her black pencil for a sapphire-blue one to create the image she had in mind. As she sipped her tea, she continued sketching, creating a lingerie piece that was different from anything else she'd designed. The gown had sheer lace cups, a v-neckline with intricate crisscross detailing in front, and a long, flowing skirt with a slit up the middle, so when a woman walked, the silky material swirled around her legs and exposed tantalizing glimpses of skin. She drew on a lacy pair of matching panties, with the same lattice details to match the top of the gown.

"Now what man in his right mind could resist a sexy outfit like that?" she murmured to herself, as she often did when she was alone and creating a design.

"I think it's more about whether he can resist the woman wearing it, not the outfit itself."

Jessica jumped at the sound of Derek's voice behind her, a startled scream erupting from her throat as she spun around, her unbound hair swirling over her shoulders. Her heart jackhammered in her chest, while he stood casually in the doorway, leaning against the frame, his arms crossed over his bare chest and his lickable abs on display. His hair was a disheveled mess, which only added to his hotness factor, and he had a lopsided smile on his gorgeous face.

She pressed a hand to her heaving chest and glared at him. "Jesus! You scared the crap out of me. Why didn't you say something so I knew you were standing there?"

"I *did* say something," he said, looking and sounding amused.

"I meant . . . never mind." She shook her head, feeling out of sorts after being startled, and it didn't help that she was distracted by Derek in a pair of cotton sweatpants hanging low on his hips. The kind that outlined any tell-tale bulge in front, and Derek's was impressive... as she'd felt for herself earlier today.

She yanked her gaze back up to his face, ignoring the sly, knowing look in his eyes. "How long have you been there watching me?"

"A while."

She straightened her silky robe and tightened the sash. "That's . . . creepy."

He shrugged unapologetically. "I liked watching you. You talk to yourself while you're drawing, and you make these cute hand gestures while you're thinking. And other times you were so intense so I just didn't want to interrupt your concentration." He pushed off the doorframe, strolled into the office and over to her drafting table, standing a respectable space away from her. "And despite what you might think, I didn't come downstairs for the sole purpose of spying on you. I was just feeling restless, and then I saw the light on, so I was curious to see what you were up to."

Fair enough. "I take it you couldn't sleep either?"

"No," he said, looking at the drawings she had pinned to a corkboard over the table of designs that she'd added to her illustrator program, most of which had already been produced as garments.

She tapped the sketch pad where she'd executed her new idea. "I had a design I couldn't get out of my head." No way would she admit thoughts of *him* had kept her awake. "What's your excuse?"

"Sleeping in a bed that's not my own," he grumbled. "I'm used to a king, not a queen. And a firmer mattress."

"Awww, poor baby. You're like the *Princess and the Pea*," she teased as she reached up and patted his stubbly cheek. "You know, being so pampered that you're sensitive to the density of a mattress. Consider your discomfort part of your penance for the weekend."

"Damn, you're ruthless," he said with a grin and a shake of his head as he glanced back at the table, to the sketch pad she'd just tapped. "So, this is the design that kept you awake?"

"Yes." She tried not to feel anxious about what he might think of the concept, but couldn't deny that his opinion mattered to her. "If I don't get it down on paper right away, I don't always remember in the morning."

He rubbed the back of his hand beneath his chin as he studied the drawing, then nodded. "I like it," he said, meeting her gaze. "It's very sexy and tastefully revealing."

She smiled. His description was exactly what she'd been attempting to achieve. "I try to keep things classy, not trashy. I'm not looking to compete with Frederick's of Hollywood."

A small frown furrowed his brow. "Who?"

"It's a lingerie brand founded by a man back in the 1940s and is more focused on the . . . explicit stuff. I just want the women who wear my designs to feel beautiful and desirable, and that means making sure that the construction of whatever I design can hold in the girls and flatters their curves," she said, knowing how difficult it was to find pretty bras and lingerie that supported her fuller breasts, or even sexy panties that covered her ass instead of ending up as a thong. "I want them to love their bodies, no matter their size or shape."

"When did you start venturing into lingerie?" he asked, sounding genuinely curious.

"I decided to give it a try about a year ago, and it's taken that long to launch Curvy Girl

Couture Lingerie. Next month is the official launch of the line." She hesitated a moment, worrying on her bottom lip, then decided to share her news, which she'd kept close to her chest even though there had been online speculation of the possible partnership. "I'm actually pretty excited, because I've been approached by a major retail brand, Belle Demoiselle, who is interested in carrying exclusive designs of my lingerie brand in their stores. We just finished a photo shoot for next month's launch, and my fingers are crossed that the launch's success will result in a contract with Belle Demoiselle."

"That's a huge accomplishment," he said, the admiration in his voice authentic and real. "I'm really proud of you."

"Thank you," she said, feeling her cheeks warm at his compliment. "That means a lot."

He leaned a hip against the drafting table, a more serious look on his face. "I know that Ben is proud of you, too . . . dare I ask about your parents?"

She sighed and absently pushed her fingers through her hair, pulling the wavy blond strands away from her face. "I think from a business standpoint, my father is impressed with what I've done. My mother? Not so much."

He blinked at her in shock. "Why wouldn't she be?"

"Despite my success, she's embarrassed. In her mind, my Curvy Girl Couture designs highlight and celebrate something she doesn't find acceptable, which is women with real curves and fuller figures." She shrugged, attempting to come off as not caring, when her mother's narrow views and criticism stung. "I've been a disappointment to her because I'm not her image of an ideal, skinny, size-two socialite daughter."

"Your mother's an idiot," he said, his gaze warm and accepting. "But parental disappointment?" he drawled in a mocking tone. "I know that curse well. My two major strikes are not following in my father's political footsteps and breaking up with Claire because I ruined the potential for both families if we'd gotten married. I swear, I will never force or guilt my kids into doing something they don't want to do."

"You want kids?" she asked, the question slipping out before she could stop it.

He raised an eyebrow. "Of course. Someday, with the right woman. Don't you want children?"

She gave him a small smile but her stomach clenched at the question. "I would love to get married and have a family, but remember that PCOS I told you about?"

He thought for a moment. "The polycystic ovary syndrome thing?"

"Yes, which comes with a bunch of other fun side effects," she said wryly. "Like a lack of ovulation. And that causes fertility issues and the possibility of me not being able to conceive a child." She couldn't hold in the sigh. "To some men, not having their own kids is a deal breaker."

She'd never had to bring up the subject with Noah, because deep inside she instinctively knew he wasn't the right man for her. It hadn't been a discussion she'd wanted to have, only for him to add that potential obstacle to all the other flaws he saw in her. God, why had she stayed with him as long as she had? And why had she just told Derek her most painful secret?

He studied her, sympathy clear in his eyes, but he didn't offer any reassurances, not that she'd expected him to. It wasn't like they were getting married and her possible fertility issues were a concern for him. They weren't even dating, and he'd made it clear he wouldn't sleep with her, so ...

"Well," she said, ready to change the subject to something less personal and painful. "Now that I've gotten my design down on paper, I'm ready to try and get some sleep and you should, too. You have a very busy day around the house tomorrow. You know, yard work, putting up the lights on the back patio, and finishing painting the trim around the outside windows." She grinned at him.

He narrowed his gaze and feigned a scowl. "Don't look so happy about it."

She laughed. "Oh, I *am* happy about watching you work hard tomorrow. I really, truly am."

And she was also looking forward to a fun evening at Club Ten29 with Derek as their personal chauffeur. She needed a night of drinking with her girlfriends, letting loose and not thinking so hard for a change. She also looked forward to dancing and flirting with a few guys—and tempting Derek's jealous streak to come out and play. He'd drawn a line he refused to cross but she hadn't, and that kiss they'd shared? She wanted a repeat.

Apparently, *she* had a naughty side. One she was coming to like. A lot.

Chapter Nine

Princess and the fucking pea. Okay, maybe Derek *was* spoiled with his king-size Elysium organic mattress in firm, but it was one of the few things he'd indulged in that made for a restful night—the opposite of what he'd gotten in Jessica's guest room bed. The mattress was probably perfectly fine for other physical activities, he thought wryly, but his back and shoulders ached as he rolled out of bed around eight, after *finally* falling asleep. A good hour after he and Jessica had parted ways around two a.m.

He did a few stretches, groaning as his vertebrae seemingly snapped back into place and his taut muscles elongated. Considering the list of chores that awaited him, he was certain more than his back would be sore by the time he was done. It was going to be a long fucking day, but there was no way he was going to slack off.

Jessica had earned, or rather bought, the right to boss him around, and if that made her happy—and clearly it would—then he was going to suck it up and put in the time and hard labor. But first, a morning run was in order to release the rest of the kinks in his body.

He changed into loose shorts, a tank top, and his running shoes and walked out of the room. Jessica's bedroom door was closed, and all was quiet inside as he walked by, so he figured she was still sleeping.

Once outside, he started out with a light jog, enjoying the cool morning air and the change of scenery. Her neighborhood was much quieter than the streets of New York City—at any time of the day or night. The houses here were midsized and quaint, with fenced-in yards and well-kept properties, and much homier than his high-rise condo. He saw kids outside playing in their front yards with their friends or dogs, and he waved to a friendly older couple enjoying a cup of coffee on their porch.

He picked up his running pace as he passed by a well-maintained park with a soccer field and marveled at all the family-owned restaurants and unique coffee shops, where people were already gathered for a Saturday morning meal or treat. There was a slow-paced, unrushed, welcoming feel to the area that Derek found incredibly relaxing and tranquil.

It was the complete opposite of what he was used to, and it was . . . nice. Knowing how wealthy Jessica's family was, and that she'd been set up with a lucrative trust fund from her grandparents as Ben had, she could have bought a place just about anywhere. Yet this was where she'd chosen to live, outside of the rush and urgency of the city. Somewhere low-key and unpretentious, just like her, he thought and couldn't help but smile.

Telling himself he couldn't avoid the inevitable list of chores forever, no matter how much he was enjoying his trek around her neighborhood, Derek headed back to Jessica's. When he entered the house, all hot and sweaty from his run, everything was still quiet, so he jogged up the steps to his room and took a cool shower.

Half an hour later, dressed in a regular T-shirt and shorts, he went downstairs to make himself a quick breakfast and came to an abrupt stop as he entered the living room.

Jessica was there, wearing a pair of black, formfitting workout pants and a sports bra that exposed a few inches of skin around her midsection. Her hair was piled on top of her head, with loose strands falling delicately around her face. Her hands and feet were planted on a rubber mat, her body positioned in an upside-down V, with her pert ass up in the air, facing him, giving him a perfect, arousing view.

He nearly swallowed his tongue, and his asshole dick twitched at the thought of coming up behind her and . . .

"What are you doing?" he blurted out, much louder than he'd intended.

"Oh, hey. Morning!" She straightened so she was standing again, smiling as she pulled out one of the Bluetooth buds from her ears. "It's yoga and that was a downward dog. I do yoga every morning. It's a great way to start the day. Plus, it helps warm up the muscles and keeps me flexible and centered."

Flexible . . . yeah, he could think of a dozen different ways to test out that theory—and immediately banished those dirty images from his mind. The yoga clearly also kept her well-toned, judging by the way her workout clothes outlined her body. She might be full-figured with soft curves, but she definitely had an hour-glass shape he found incredibly alluring and sexy.

"Everything okay?" She was looking at him, head tipped to the side, eyes full of concern.

Shit. He'd been staring at her for longer than what was appropriate. "Uh, yeah," he stammered, knowing he sounded like an idiot. Not to mention he was lusting over someone he couldn't have.

He scrambled for a change of subject. "Want breakfast?"

"No, thank you." She lowered herself into another yoga pose, one knee bent and her arms straight out by her sides. "I already had my morning protein shake."

He nodded. "Okay, then I'll grab a bite to

eat and get started outside finishing what the contractors didn't get done."

"Sounds good," she said, stretching both arms above her head, which only served to draw his attention to her full breasts, outlined beneath the sports bra she wore. "I have some things to do inside, so I'll come out in a little bit to check on how things are going."

He gave her a playful salute, then went into the kitchen to rummage through her refrigerator for breakfast. He found eggs, cheese, and mushrooms and made himself an omelet, which he washed down with a glass of orange juice.

As he walked out the slider to the backyard, he pulled up the text message Jessica had sent with the to-do list, making a mental note of what the contractors were able to do yesterday and what was still left to be completed. He started with the trim around the outside windows, spending hours painting them a soft gray shade to offset the darker gray siding on her house.

When that was done and he was able to check that item off his list, he moved on to stringing the lights along the patio pergola. He'd just opened the first box of lights when

Jessica stepped outside, now wearing a bathing suit—a sexy one-piece that was tight across the bust and abdomen, with a flirty little skirt that skimmed just the tops of her thighs. She had on big, white-framed sunglasses and flip-flops, clearly heading out to the pool, while he continued to labor away.

"I take it *your* chores are done?" he asked.

"Yep." She grinned at him. "I thought I'd come out and enjoy the nice weather and supervise."

He picked up the string of lights. "How would you like these put up?"

"I don't know." She waved her hand up toward the lattice opening. "I guess kind of crisscrossing back and forth?"

Well, that wasn't specific at all, but he had an idea of what she meant. "Okay, got it," he said in a wry tone.

As he opened the package of hooks, he watched Jessica walk through the small yard to a nearby shed, enjoying the subtle sway of her hips as she moved. She went inside, then returned with a blown-up floating device that looked like a lounge chair. She put it into the shallow end of the pool, then managed to sit on top of the floating chair without tipping over.

With a cheeky grin, she treated him to a little finger wave. "Don't worry about me. I can swim."

Clearly, he'd been staring at her too long, *again*, so he shook his head and got to work. Using a ladder, he started at one end of the patio cover and began hanging the lights on hooks he screwed into the beams, doing a criss-cross method as she'd requested. He left a bit of slack so that the bulbs hung in a low, symmetrical pattern along the pergola. Nearly an hour later, he was almost finished when she piped up.

"Hey, can you drape that last string of lights a little bit more to the left?" she asked as she lazily skimmed her fingers in the pool water. "They look off from here."

He didn't think so, but it was her patio, not his. "Sure."

He rearranged the ladder beneath the hooks and did as she asked, and just when he finished and stepped off the ladder, she sighed and said, "No, I think it was better the way it was before, but maybe a little more to the right?"

He glanced her way, trying not to glare at her uncertain directions. "Are you *sure*?"

She gave him an impish smile. "Yeah, I think so."

He turned and rolled his eyes, then back up the ladder he went, repositioning the lights and making sure he got her approval before he climbed back down.

When both feet were back on the patio, she made a *hmm* sound, then said, "Can you make it so it's not sagging in the middle part of the pergola?"

He clenched his jaw in annoyance. It *wasn't* sagging, not from his perspective, and he wanted to yell, *Make up your fucking mind*, but damned if he'd give her the satisfaction. He knew she was doing this to exasperate him and enjoying every moment, and if it made up for his past infraction in her mind, then he'd grit his teeth and do it. Which he did.

"That's much better," she praised him while clapping her hands. "Good job!"

What am I, a dog? He rolled his eyes once

129

more as he cleaned up the boxes and the rest of the packaging, throwing it all in the outdoor trash. He mentally crossed that job off his list and brought out the hedge trimmer to work on the shrubs, already feeling his shoulders beginning to ache.

"Before you start doing the shrubs, could you bring me a glass of iced tea, please?" she asked oh-so-sweetly. "There's a pitcher of it in the refrigerator."

"I would *love* to," he drawled, not bothering to hide his sarcasm, and went to do her bidding.

The only upside to delivering her drink was when she paddled to the edge of the pool and he crouched down to hand her the plastic tumbler, which she took. He received a nice eyeful of her cleavage and didn't bother to hide his appreciative stare. And when he lifted his gaze to her face, he didn't miss the knowing smirk on her lips that told him she was deliberately teasing and tempting him.

He stood back up, looking down at her with his hands on his hips. "Anything else before I get back to work, princess?"

She took a sip of her tea and grinned. "No, I'm good for now. Thank you."

He looked at all her pale, smooth skin on

display. It wasn't an overly hot day, but the last thing he wanted was her fair skin to burn. "Did you put on sunscreen?" he asked.

She lowered her sunglasses and batted her lashes at him. "Yes, *Daddy*, I did."

She was mocking him, but that word coming from her mouth gave *daddy* a whole different meaning, one that made a fair amount of lust course through his blood. And by the wicked gleam in her eyes, she knew it, too, the minx. Despite having half a dozen dirty remarks on the tip of his tongue, he ignored her comment, turned, and returned to the yard work with a hard, aching dick.

He endured another hour of her bossing him around. *I think you missed a spot over there, Derek. Trim the hedges a bit lower, Derek. Make sure you don't clip the rose bushes too short please, Derek.* With her excessive demands and adjustments, she was making it take twice as long for him to get anything done, and he'd had it.

He was hot and sweaty and feeling annoyed and cantankerous. Not even her sexy bathing suit eased his frustration. "Jessica!" he finally shouted. "Let me at least finish each

131

chore before you start criticizing my work." He freely admitted he was no landscaper, but she was driving him insane.

"Oh, I'm sorry." She pressed a hand to her chest, feigning contrition. "Am I being too nit-picky?"

He narrowed his gaze on the slight, sinful curve of her lips. Oh, she wasn't sorry at all. With gritted teeth, he watched her float in the deep end of the pool, not a care in the world, like a princess on her throne as she delegated to her minion—which, at the moment, was him.

Done being bossed around, he set down the trimmer and crossed the yard, kicking off his shoes and removing his socks as he neared the pool. Her gaze settled on him as he ripped off his damp T-shirt and tossed it aside, leaving him in just his shorts.

Her lips parted—which almost made him grin. "What are . . . you . . . you doing?" she stuttered as he drew closer, while he enjoyed watching as she finally realized he'd gained some power in their little dynamic. "You're not done with the trimming!"

"I am for now." He continued toward her,

even as she tried to paddle away from the deep end with her hands. "I think I need to cool off."

Grinning, he gave himself a small running start, and just as he reached the edge of the pool, he jumped up, tucking his legs beneath him with his arms holding them in place as he catapulted himself toward the deep end.

"Derek . . . Nooo!" Jessica yelled.

It was too late to stop him and all he felt was smug satisfaction as he dive-bombed into the cool water—creating a huge splash that produced a turbulent wave strong enough to tip over Jessica's floatie, unceremoniously dumping her into the pool.

He rose to the surface at the same time she did, a good six feet away, with her sputtering for air and staring at him in shock. Her sunglasses were gone, and half of her wet hair had come loose from the clip on her head. She looked adorable, even with that peeved look on her face.

"That was a total jerk move," she said, using the palm of her hand to splash water toward him, but he was too far away to hit him square on.

"Yeah, well, you deserved it after bossing

me around all afternoon, just to make things more difficult. So this time, maybe *I* wanted a bit of payback."

He swam toward her and she backed away, turning so she could move faster. He kept it up, slowly, deliberately, *playfully* stalking her around the pool. Every time she looked back to see where he was, her eyes flashed not with panic but with a goddamn gleam of fire. Daring him to catch her. She was such a tease, and he couldn't resist the chase, his body rock hard at the thought of what he'd do to her if he captured her at last.

She dipped beneath the surface and kicked off, heading to the opposite side of the pool, but he was faster, and when she popped back out of the water, he was right there. She let out a startled scream and backed up, cornering herself against the edge of the pool.

With a warning smirk, he closed the distance and braced his hands on either side of her body. "Gotcha," he murmured, all the pent-up sexual tension heating up between them again.

She licked her pink, wet lips. "Now that you have me, what are you going to do with me?" she whispered, looking up at him with water droplets sparkling on her lashes.

His gaze fell to her sassy mouth. He knew what he *wanted* to do, and he was also well aware that Jessica was all but inviting him to kiss her again. Those lips beckoned to him, and desire churned hot and heavy in his veins— despite his vow to keep his hands, mouth, and other body parts to himself.

Clearly, he hadn't thought through catching and trapping her, or her cheeky *what are you going to do* taunt.

Her question haunted him and he forced out his reply. "Not a fucking thing," he said, regret in his tone as he pushed himself away, not missing her disappointment. "I need to finish up the yard work, and you should probably go take a shower and get ready for your girls' night out."

"Yeah, I'll do that," she said, turning around and wading out of the pool.

Water dripped off her curves, and everything in him wanted to scream, *Screw it* and pounce on her. Take what he wanted. What she offered. Because resisting was torment for

135

them both, but he was the one enforcing the "no touching" rules.

But he didn't do any of those things.

As she walked away without looking back, he couldn't help but wonder how long he was going to last before his good intentions went to hell and his control snapped.

And what would happen then?

Chapter Ten

Jessica took a long, hot shower, shampooing the chlorine out of her hair and using a body scrub to exfoliate her skin. All the while, she tried not to let her frustration with Derek get the best of her or dampen her enthusiasm for the evening's fun she planned to have with her friends at Club Ten29.

This afternoon, she'd definitely enjoyed the easy flirtation and light banter between them until things had taken a very tempting turn in the pool. He'd come so close to kissing her again, and a fluttering sensation took up residence in her stomach at the memory of how desperately she'd ached to feel his lips on hers a second time . . . only to be denied.

She exhaled a heavy sigh as she shaved her legs. Obviously, Derek had more willpower than she did, and a part of her couldn't help but wonder what it would take for him to step over that line he'd drawn and break his own self-imposed rules. She wasn't sure, but tonight she refused to dwell on the push-pull sexual tension sparking between them and planned to enjoy a night out clubbing. And if that meant tempting and teasing Derek a bit more to test those boundaries, so be it.

She finished up in the shower, and since she still had a few hours before they had to pick up Avery and Maddie, she put on a comfortable sundress and retreated to her office. There was always work to do and she needed to handle emails from the social media manager she'd hired to help elevate her business's profile. She approved the most recent content and campaigns, reviewed the analytics, and authorized the ideas and videos that had been presented for next month's launch of Curvy Girl Couture Lingerie.

By four p.m., she decided to wrap things up

and make dinner for Derek. It was the least she could do, considering he'd spent the entire day outside finishing up her to-do list and was probably hungry.

Just as she pulled the baked salmon, roasted vegetables, and potatoes from the oven, Derek strode into the kitchen from the backyard, dirty and sweaty from hours spent working outdoors. Yet he still managed to look hot and gorgeous. It so wasn't fair.

He walked to the sink to wash his hands and forearms. "That smells amazing," he said with a groan. "I was expecting to have to make some kind of dinner tonight as part of my penance but I'm grateful to be off the hook."

Grinning at him, she served up each of their plates, giving him a more ample portion, and took them to the table. "I'm not a complete slave driver."

He snorted. "I beg to differ," he said, drying his hands with a paper towel, then grimaced as he glanced down at the dirt on his T-shirt and shorts. "And I really should go shower because I'm absolutely filthy."

Shaking her head, she pointed to the table. "Sit and eat while it's hot and fresh," she ordered, then poured them each a glass of iced tea and sat down next to him.

Obviously starved, he dove right into the meal, polishing off half of it before he took a long drink of his tea then glanced at her. "Nikki called me a while ago to chortle in delight over my situation as your manservant, and I made the mistake of telling her I was chauffeuring you and your friends to the club tonight."

Jessica swallowed a tender bite of salmon and tipped her head curiously. "Why was that a mistake?"

"Because she insisted on going, too." He gave her an apologetic look. "I hope you don't mind."

"Of course not," she said. "Nikki is great. The more the merrier, I say."

He smiled, looking relieved that she was okay with his sister coming with them. "Thank you. Nikki doesn't have a lot of close friends, so I appreciate you letting her join you and *your* friends. And, as your designated driver, I figure I'll be able to hang out with Asher while you girls do your thing since I know that clubbing isn't his idea of an exciting night out, either."

They finished eating dinner and Derek

insisted on doing the dishes, so Jessica let him, since she knew it was going to take her a while to get ready. Up in her bathroom, she curled her hair into soft waves and left it cascading down her back, then applied more dramatic makeup than her normal daily routine. Darker shadows, a little shimmer below her brows, and kohl liner with a sexy winged curve at the outer corner of each eye. She finished off the look with a luminous berry-bronze shade of lipstick.

Then, she changed into her outfit for the evening—skinny faux-leather pants and a metallic rose camisole. She wouldn't deny she'd maybe, possibly, chosen the pieces to grab Derek's attention. Thin straps crisscrossed along her back, and the loosely draped cowl-neck bodice exposed a hint of cleavage while leaving a whole lot of skin still bare. She slipped into her favorite four-inch strappy heels and added a pair of dangly earrings and a detailed crystal wrist cuff that Avery had given her as a birthday gift.

Grabbing her small purse, she folded a leather jacket over her arm just in case she needed it later and headed downstairs while texting Maddie and Avery to let them know she was leaving and to be ready.

Derek sat on the couch in the living room, waiting for her. Freshly showered, he wore black pants and a plum-colored long-sleeved button-down dress shirt. He was also texting on his phone, and he absently glanced up when she walked in—then did a comical double take when he saw her.

His eyes darkened possessively, making something deliciously arousing swirl in her stomach. But a few seconds later, he pushed to his feet, his gaze narrowing as it slowly traveled from her head to her toes, then back up again, searing her with his hot perusal.

His jaw clenched tight. "If you walk into the club wearing that outfit, I guarantee that at least half of the guys there are only going to be thinking about one thing."

She *innocently* blinked at him. "And what's that?"

"Taking you home with them and fucking you," he said, his voice a low growl.

If he meant to shock her, his brazen comment had the opposite effect, and instead, she wondered if he was having those same thoughts. She sure as hell hoped so.

She lifted a shoulder in a shrug. "Good. It's been a while and there's nothing wrong with a one-night stand to scratch that itch," she said, managing to hold back a smirk that would give away her giddiness at his obvious jealousy.

"Not on my goddamn watch," he said irritably, his gaze dropping to her loose-fitting neckline and the cleavage on display. "You need to change."

She rolled her eyes at his caveman attitude. "Into what? A burlap sack?"

"Preferably," he gritted out.

She laughed in amusement. "Sorry, mine's at the cleaners," she said in a cheeky tone, then headed for the front door. "Maddie and Avery are ready to be picked up, so let's go," she said when he didn't immediately follow her.

He swore beneath his breath, and it took effort to continue to hold back her grin. *He* was the one who refused to touch her or give in to the undeniable attraction between them. Yet he clearly didn't want anyone else making moves on her, either. Not that there was anyone else she wanted.

Hmm. The notion put a little pep in her step and filled her head with all the fun ways she could rile him up tonight to see what happened.

This evening might be more interesting than she'd anticipated.

Chapter Eleven

After picking up Maddie and Avery, Derek drove them to Club Ten29 in downtown Manhattan. Though it was only seven o'clock and early in terms of clubbing time, a long line of people already waited to get inside. He wasn't surprised. The place was both popular and exclusive. He drove up to the valet, and once he and the girls exited the SUV, Derek swapped his keys for a ticket from the attendant.

He'd received a text from Asher, who was already inside with Nikki, waiting in the VIP area—a perk courtesy of their friend and one of the owners, Jason Dare. Asher had taken one look at the line around the side of the building and called, pulling strings so they didn't have to wait hours for a chance to get inside the trendy nightclub. Derek should have thought of doing the same, but his mind had turned to mush the second he'd seen Jessica walk down the stairs in that sexy fuck-me outfit. His teeth hadn't unclenched since.

Escorting the three chatty women to the door, Derek gave the security guy his name and they were immediately granted access. As soon as they walked inside the modern, upscale club, upbeat techno music pulsed through him. Colorful LED wall lights illuminated the spacious main area, which also included two bars, seating areas for socializing, and a massive dance floor.

The lower level was already filled with people, which made him feel claustrophobic. "You want to head up to the VIP area? Asher and Nikki are waiting," he asked the women, hoping they'd agree so he could keep a closer eye on Jessica.

She gave him a full-wattage smile. "No, we want to be where the fun is."

He rolled his eyes. Of course she did.

Jessica glanced up to the second level and

waved to Nikki, who was sitting at a table with Asher that overlooked the bar and dance area, and gestured for her to join them.

Once she made her way downstairs, his sister let him know Asher remained at the VIP table. One glance told Derek that Asher kept a close eye on his fiancée from where he was sitting. Jessica, meanwhile, looped her arm through Nikki's and the four women headed toward the bar for a drink.

Derek quickly scanned the area. Just as he thought, the wolves were out tonight, and Jessica's sexy outfit, combined with her gorgeous face and body, attracted more than a few interested male stares. Avery, Maddie, and Nikki were also dressed up, but they weren't in clothing that showed nearly as much skin, which made Jessica stand out even more, and another round of annoyance settled inside him.

With her gorgeous blond hair hanging down her back, those luscious curves outlined in formfitting leather pants, and the fuck-me heels that seemed to lengthen the legs he wanted wrapped around his waist, she was going to wreak havoc with his sanity tonight.

He shot a warning glare at every guy in the

vicinity, which was ridiculous, considering no one was paying *him* any attention. He did a quick sweep of the sitting area, then back-tracked when he saw a pair of women he recognized. Peyton and Tiffany, two of Claire's close girlfriends, were huddled around a table, their eyes watching the other girls at the bar. He searched for his ex, didn't find her, and assumed she hadn't joined her friends, causing him to exhale a sigh of relief. She was the last person he wanted to deal with tonight.

Determined to let Jessica have her fun, he made his way up to the VIP area and took a seat beside Asher, grateful it was a bit quieter up there. After greeting the other man, he ordered a ginger beer mojito mocktail from the waitress, then fell into an easy conversation with his friend.

"Sorry that my sister dragged you out tonight," Derek said in a wry tone, certain that Asher could have found many other relaxing ways to spend the evening.

Asher shrugged, though he had a smile on his face. "Whatever makes her happy."

Derek barely refrained from rolling his eyes. Yeah, the man was completely and totally whipped. "Well, witnessing my role as Jessica's manservant clearly makes Nikki happy."

"True," Asher admitted with a smirk. "Along with being around people she likes and trusts. She doesn't go out often, so I'm more than willing to indulge her when it's something she wants to do."

The waitress delivered his order, setting the glass down next to Asher's. Derek took a sip of the lightweight drink, immediately wishing for a much stronger beverage.

"You know I would have ordered Dirty Dare Vodka if I wasn't designated driver tonight," he said of Asher's liquor brand.

"Same here," Asher replied, lifting his own nonalcoholic drink with a slight grimace. "But someone has to stay clear-headed in a place like this, with men like *that*."

He pointed to the lower level, and Derek's gaze automatically found the women. They each had a cocktail in hand and were already surrounded by vultures. He watched as four men talked to each woman. Nikki kept a discreet distance while attempting to listen to the man who'd chosen her. Maddie, Avery, and Jessica openly flirted with the other guys, with

Jessica flipping her hair over her shoulder and laughing at something one of the idiots said.

"That shit doesn't bother you?" he asked Asher.

"Damn straight it does. Watching some guy flirt with my fiancée pisses me off, but it's a club, she's beautiful, and guys are going to try and hit on her." It didn't escape Derek's notice that Asher's knuckles had turned white around his glass. "As long as no one touches her or puts her in an uncomfortable situation, I won't have to break any jaws."

"Wow, that's so fucking logical and reasonable," Derek muttered, which was the opposite of how *he* was feeling.

Asher smirked. "Well, that and she *persuaded* me to leave the caveman routine at home so she could enjoy the night out."

Derek glanced at Asher curiously. "Persuaded?"

Asher laughed, the sound low and dirty. "Trust me, you don't want to know."

Catching his meaning, Derek put up a hand and quickly said, "You're right, I don't."

They continued to watch the women, and after a while, Asher spoke again. "I'm not sure if Nikki told you, but your mother has been trying to reach her, leaving messages and texts," he said, finishing his drink and signaling to the waitress for another.

Derek stiffened. Nikki had been tortured enough by their mother. "What for?" he asked, doing nothing to hide the sarcasm in his tone. "To apologize for being such a bitch and maybe, actually, show a little humility and motherly love?"

Asher barked out a laugh. "Hardly. Your sister won't take her calls, so Collette has left voice mail messages trying to guilt her into attending your father's upcoming political fundraiser next weekend, to 'show a united front' so you all look like one big happy family for the press and his donors."

Which was all a fucking façade. They weren't a happy family, and their mother's aspirations—which exceeded their father's—were the reason. But Collette Bettencourt was all about keeping up pretenses, even at the expense of her children's well-being. For once, Nikki wasn't allowing their mother to manipulate her into doing what she wanted.

Derek stood by Nikki's decision and agreed

with her reasons to sever ties with their parents, but he carried his own guilt for being in contact with them. He'd definitely put boundaries up with his mother, but he'd never had antagonistic issues with his father. Though he viewed the man as weak, he couldn't bring himself to abandon him.

He exhaled a breath and scrubbed a hand along his jaw. "I'm not going to lie. It feels like I'm betraying Nikki by attending the fundraiser, but I agreed months ago. Not for my mother but to support my father."

Asher nodded in understanding. "Nikki doesn't blame you," he assured Derek. "This is her issue, and she doesn't expect you to be estranged from your parents on her behalf."

Which would be incredibly easy to do when it came to his mother, Derek thought. Not so much with his dad.

Asher must have sensed his unease because he changed the conversation to business, then sports. They discussed the upcoming football season and debated which teams would end up at the Super Bowl, but their attention never wavered from the girls in the main club area.

A few hours passed, and Derek tried to

keep that green-eyed monster from emerging as he watched Jessica flirt with the same guy over the long night and order a few more drinks. She laughed with abandon, continued to toss her hair in a sexy, seductive manner, and put her hand briefly on the other man's arm. Then there was the dancing and the way she moved her body with confidence to the rhythm of the music. The more she drank, the more uninhibited her dance moves seemed to become.

She was having fun, Derek repeatedly reminded himself and let her enjoy the evening despite the possessiveness escalating inside him . . . until the other man put his hands on her waist. Jessica immediately made it clear his advances were unwanted, removing his hands from her waist, and her hips, and her ass . . . all with a playful laugh or a smile.

But the asshole wasn't taking the hint.

"Jesus, you look like you're going to blow a fucking gasket," Asher noted, his tone amused.

"That dick she's with is mauling her," he fumed, his entire body stiff with irritation.

Asher arched a brow. "Mauling, really? She seems to be handling herself just fine."

Derek gave him a pointed look. "Would

you be saying that if it was Nikki in that situation?"

"No, because Nikki is my fiancée, which gives me the right to kick any guy's ass who touches her."

Derek's jaw clenched so tight he was certain he was going to crack his molars. "Are you saying I have no right to interfere?"

Asher shrugged, a sudden smirk on his face. "Depends on if you're staking a claim." He paused a beat. "Are you?"

Fuck yes, Derek wanted to roar as he watched as the guy, yet again, tried to pull Jessica against his chest. "No," he gritted out. "I'm protecting her from assholes who want to take advantage of her."

"Okay, yeah, sure." Amusement flickered in Asher's eyes. "Then go do your thing, *caveman*. I'll just sit here and watch the show."

"Fuck you," Derek said, ignoring his friend's loud laughter as he jumped up from his chair and made his way down to the lower level.

Getting through the crush of people around the bar and pushing his way to the dance floor wasn't easy, but he was determined. When he reached Jessica and her dance partner, who'd managed to secure a hand around her waist to keep their bodies flush, Derek had to resist the urge to throat-punch the bastard for leering at her tits with pure lust in his eyes.

He grabbed the douchebag's arm and flung it off Jessica, then shoved his shoulder, causing him to stumble backward. "Get your fucking hands off her," Derek said, a heated warning in his voice. "She's with me."

The guy eyed Derek up and down, his glassy eyes telling Derek he'd had too much to drink. "Who are you?" he sneered. "Her brother?"

Derek's hand curled into a fist. "No, I'm her goddamn boyfriend," he said, barely recognizing the feral tone of his voice. "And unless you want to leave here without your teeth and all your extremities intact, I suggest you walk away. Now."

"I didn't know." The guy lifted his hands in a show of neutrality as he backed up farther. "No chick is worth this. She's all yours."

"Damn right she is," Derek said, watching the other man retreat before glancing back at

Jessica, whose glossy lips were curved into a delighted smile.

"My boyfriend, hmm?" She stepped closer and slid a hand along his chest, ignoring the couples dancing around them, including her friends, who were too busy to notice the scene he'd made.

Even through his shirt, her touch made his skin catch fire and his dick stir in his pants, and he caught her wrist, gently pulling it away. "He was disrespecting your boundaries, and it worked to make him leave you alone." *That was his excuse and he was sticking to it.*

"Yes, he was," she agreed, and as soon as he released her hand to escort her off the dance floor, she lifted her arms so that they circled his neck and brazenly pressed her body to his. "And I would have kneed him in the dick if he did anything that made me uncomfortable."

Her hips shifted against his, a slow, not-so-subtle gyration his cock couldn't ignore. "I doubt you're that coordinated at the moment." He caught her hips in his hands to keep her from rubbing up against him so sinuously. "How many drinks have you had?"

She lifted one of her hands from his

shoulder and squinted at it, trying to use her fingers to count. "Mmm, four, maybe five?" she said, a slight slur in her voice as she leaned closer, a sexy, playful smile on her lips. "But don't worry about me having too much to drink. I have a designated driver."

He hated to admit it, but she looked adorable, and he forcibly swallowed back a laugh. "I think it's time to take you home," he said, trying to sound stern.

She shook her head, causing all that silky blond hair to shift across her bare back and her breasts to jiggle against his chest. "Nope. I'm not ready yet." She cast him a coy, tipsy look. "And guess what, knight in shining armor. Now that you've chased off my dance partner, that forces *you* to take his place."

Oh, hell. "Yeah, no, that's not my thing."

Her lashes fell half-mast, her expression sultry and determined. "But it's *my* thing and my weekend," she reminded him, then slowly slid her arms from around his neck and stepped back. "So if you're not interested, I'll just find another dance partner who is, because I'm not ready to go home."

Fuck. He didn't doubt she'd make good on

her threat. Before she could do just that, he hooked his arm around the waist and brought her flush against his body. His conscience told him he should have let her go. That same conscience reminded him it was his job to look out for her, to not let her go find a fuck buddy for the night.

Especially when he wanted that to be him.

A small triumphant spark lit her eyes, and it took all his control to resist the urge to smack her ass, *hard*, for being so full of sass.

God, she was such a handful, so damn bold and daring, and those personality traits exhilarated him. She was sweet, sassy, and delightfully unpredictable. Unlike the staid women he was used to, Jessica kept him on his toes and had his blood pumping. And that was before this evening. With a few drinks under her belt, her inhibitions melted away and she tempted him like he'd never been tempted before.

Knowing it would only drive him insane to watch her dance with another man, he stayed right where he was and allowed her to drive him crazy in a whole different way. He loosened his grip so she could dance but she had an agenda of her own. She looped her arms around his neck and pulled him close, moving to the music, her warm, curvy body rubbing against him in time to the pulsing beat.

She tossed her hair, turning around to do a sexy shimmy and backing into him until her ass nestled perfectly against his groin and the unmistakably stiff erection in his pants. Without thinking, he pressed a hand to her stomach and ground against her backside, feeling her shiver against him, as if she was just as desperate as he was for more.

She spun to face him, leaning against his chest. With her mouth inches below his, she parted her lips and the temptation was too great. His brain short-circuited and, done resisting what he wanted so fucking badly, he didn't hesitate to take what she was offering. Threading both hands into her hair, he dipped his head and captured her mouth with his. She tasted like the fruity cocktails she'd drunk and he needed more. Apparently, so did she. She gripped his shirt, her body went lax, soft, and needy, and he felt a moan of pure need vibrate against his lips.

He swept his tongue deep inside her waiting mouth and desire detonated through his veins. His stomach muscles tightened, his dick throbbed, and the thoughts in his mind spun in a dozen dirty, filthy directions—all inappropriate in a public setting. Probably in any setting but he wasn't going to think about that now.

He'd seen other couples kissing at the club, but he wanted to fucking *consume* Jessica. He wanted to strip her bare, taste every inch of her skin, and imprint his scent on her. To make her his like a goddamn *caveman*.

The song ended long enough to snap some sense back into him. He stared down at Jessica's flushed face. Her eyes were dilated with desire, her lips parted, and she was breathing heavily—like he'd just fucked her instead of danced with her.

He swallowed back a groan. "We're done here. I'm taking you home."

She nodded and didn't argue—seemingly still stunned by that kiss. "Okay, but I'm, umm, going to go to the ladies' room first."

He nodded, needing the time to pull himself together as well. "I'll wait for you at the bar."

Derek headed in that direction, catching

sight of Claire's two girlfriends watching him, their heads close together as they talked. They'd probably witnessed everything that had happened between himself and Jessica out on the dance floor—not that he gave a damn.

Withdrawing his phone, he typed out a text to Asher. *Would you mind dropping off Maddie and Avery when you and Nikki leave? Jessica had too much to drink and I'm taking her home.*

Less than a minute later, Asher replied. *I'll take them, but now* you *fucking owe me again. PS: Looks like you staked that claim.*

Asher was such an asshole for pointing out his possessive behavior, Derek thought with a shake of his head.

As for owing him . . . their debt kept going back and forth. This past summer, Derek had convinced Asher to take Nikki to his private island after her scandal by reminding Asher of a favor Derek had once done for him. Asher helping Nikki had ended up very well for them both, in Derek's mind, making them even. Now Derek owed Asher again.

He refused to touch the claim-staking comment. Not when his head was still spinning from their time on the dance floor.

Instead, Derek texted back, *I'm sure you'll make me pay,* and pocketed his cellphone.

He ordered a glass of water from the bartender for Jessica and kept an eye on the ladies' room, that hot kiss in the forefront of his mind. Along with the fact that he'd not just initiated it, he'd been reluctant to end it.

He no longer had to ask himself what he was doing with Jessica. He wanted her and was done trying to thwart their mutual attraction. He'd just have to live with the consequences of his actions—his relationship with her brother, his friend and business partner—later. Because watching Jessica tonight had enlightened him. What he wanted with Jessica was more than just sex, and she was worth any risk that came with pursuing her.

But there was also no way he'd do anything beyond that dance floor kiss when she was as intoxicated as she was tonight. And he had no doubt his little spitfire wouldn't be taking his decision well.

Chapter Twelve

Jessica finished up in the restroom, and as she was washing her hands, she glanced up and saw her reflection in the decorative mirror above the sink. Her cheeks were a rosy hue, due in no small part to the deep, demanding kiss Derek had shockingly planted on her lips. She pressed her hands to her hot cheeks, her senses reeling. From his possessive behavior when he'd chased off her dance partner to his desire to leave the club with her now, she was facing an entirely different Derek.

And now that he'd kissed her again, she wasn't going to let him backpedal or claim that keeping his hands to himself was the right and respectful thing to do. She was done with the noble and honorable Derek. She wanted the possessive, dominant one. She'd already bought his full attention this weekend, but his actions on the dance floor had nothing to do with the auction and everything to do with their mutual attraction. In her mind, a fun, sexy little hookup wasn't going to hurt anyone.

All she wanted was one night of incredible pleasure with the man she'd had a crush on since she'd been a teenager. No one had to know about their affair but the two of them, which eliminated any concern he might have about her brother—as his best friend *or* business partner. It wasn't like she was asking for a commitment of any kind, and she was more than capable of keeping their fling a secret.

She dried off her hands with a few paper towels, amused by the fact that Derek believed she was drunk. Yes, it was true that she'd had about five drinks throughout the evening. Two cocktails until she had a nice little buzz to start off the night, then the rest all nonalcoholic.

She was actually quite coherent, something she wasn't ready to reveal to Derek just yet. She'd rather have some fun with the fact that he believed she was tipsy, which allowed her a bit of freedom to be more brazen and uninhibited on the drive home. She was going to get a little handsy and ramp up the flirtation, she thought, smiling to herself. She'd tease him, tempt him, and let him squirm, trying to deflect her sexy advances until he could no longer resist her.

She fluffed her hair with her fingers, readjusted the neckline of her camisole so the top swells of her breasts were on display, then strolled back into the club and toward the bar where he said he'd be waiting.

He zeroed in on her as she approached, his gaze dropping to the cleavage she'd exposed, then to the deliberate sway of her hips, before bouncing back up to her face, a scowl marring his brows.

Reaching for a glass of water, he handed it to her. "Drink this so you stay hydrated. It will help dilute the alcohol in your system."

She gave him a slow, languid blink and took the glass from his hands. "Yes, sir," she murmured, almost laughing as she watched his eyes go dark and hot.

She drank about half the water, set the glass

back on the bar top, then intentionally leaned against the front of his body as if she couldn't stand straight on her own. He caught her around the waist, and she toyed with the collar of his shirt as she tipped her head up to meet his gaze.

"I'm ready for you to take me home . . . sir," she said, infusing a husky quality to her voice.

The clench of his jaw told her that he didn't miss the innuendo in her words, but he kept himself under control and began escorting her through the crowd. "Let's go."

"Wait, aren't we taking Maddie and Avery with us?" she asked.

"No." He shook his head and kept directing her toward the exit. "I already asked Asher to drop them off when he and Nikki leave."

Which meant she now had Derek all to herself, she thought happily.

She tried to slow him down, just to make things a little more difficult on him. "Why are you in such a rush to get me out of here?"

He tightened his arm around her waist and pulled her closer to his side as he navigated through another cluster of people. "Because I think you've had more than enough to drink, *and way too much fun*, and it's time to call it a night."

She pouted up at him. "What if I'm not done having fun?"

"Trust me, you'll thank me in the morning for not letting you overindulge any more than you already have."

She sighed, purposely sounding displeased with his decision but relenting. "All right. Whatever you say."

He blew out a breath, obviously relieved she wasn't going to give him a hard time, and she behaved herself until they were in his SUV, buckled up, and driving toward her home. Once she'd lulled him into a false sense of security, making him believe she was going to be good, she leaned across the console—as much as she could with her seat belt on—and playfully walked her fingers up his thigh while pressing her breasts against his arm.

Lips near his ear, she murmured, "So, I was thinking about the boyfriend thing you mentioned . . . does that come with benefits?"

His body stiffened at her insinuation, and before she could skim her fingers along the front of his pants, he pushed her hand back down to his knee. "No. Not tonight," he said gruffly.

She found his choice of words interesting. "Too bad. I could really, really use the benefits part of having a boyfriend." She exhaled a sigh of disappointment that ruffled the hair by his ear and trailed her fingers right back up his leg again. "I know your cock doesn't vibrate like my battery-operated boyfriend does, but from what I've felt, a few times now, you would more than get the job done," she said and palmed his erection, giving it an experimental squeeze.

A low groan rumbled in his throat, and his hands tightened on the steering wheel.

She stroked him lazily through the fabric of his slacks.

"*Jessica.*" Her name came out as a stern warning.

"Hmmm?" she asked innocently.

"I'm *driving*," he said through gritted teeth.

She swallowed back a laugh. "And doing a damn good job of it," she said, her words slow and languid.

She traced a finger around what felt like the very large head of his cock. At the feel of him, big and thick, desire rushed through her, and she squeezed her thighs together, searching for relief but realizing her mistake when another wave of need raced through her.

Forcing her focus back to him, she squeezed once more. "Don't mind me. I'm just sizing things up."

"*Fuck*," he growled and pulled her hand off his erection. This time, he trapped her palm beneath his thigh, assuring she couldn't touch him again. "You're going to cause us to get into a fucking accident."

"Hmm, then maybe you need to work on your self-control."

He turned his head and gaped at her, and she blinked at him guilelessly. She had to admit that being "pretend drunk" was fun. It allowed her to be far more shameless and brazen than she'd ever allowed herself to be before, and she found it liberating to be playful and openly sexual with a man. But he was right, she needed to be more careful about touching him while he was driving.

"It's okay," she said, not finished toying with him verbally. "No need to be embarrassed." She spoke in a soothing tone. "Noah, my previous boyfriend, had an issue with premature ejaculation—"

He nearly slammed on the brakes when a streetlight turned red. They came to a jarring stop and he barked out, "I don't have an issue with stamina."

She deliberately widened her eyes at his outburst. "Oh, you don't have to get upset about it. I just thought . . ."

"How about you just *stop* thinking for a while," he suggested. "*And* talking."

"You don't have to be so grumpy about it," she huffed, then turned her head toward the passenger window to hide her grin.

She gave him a short reprieve for the rest of the drive to her place but made sure to sway and stumble like someone still tipsy so he'd help her to the front door, then up the stairs to her bedroom. He switched on the nightstand lamp, and once she sat down on her bed, he started making a hasty retreat out of there.

"Where are you going?" she asked.

He stopped, turned, and put his hands on his lean hips. "To my *own* room."

"Wait," she said breathlessly and flopped back onto her mattress, her fingers fumbling with the button on her pants. "I need you to help me pull these leather pants off. I don't think I can do it myself." She wasn't lying. The formfitting material was a bitch to take off, but she definitely had other motives tonight.

He closed his eyes for a moment, and she realized that this was it. This playful façade was about to turn very real, and now that the moment had arrived, she couldn't deny she was nervous. She'd never seduced a man before, and while she had no doubts that Derek wanted her, there was a tiny bit of old insecurity swirling around in her stomach because he was *Derek*. The only man that truly mattered.

He exhaled a deep breath then returned to the bed. She lifted one foot and treated him to an impish smile. "Can you take off my shoes, please?"

He paused, then unbuckled the strappy heels and let each one fall to the floor while she unzipped her pants, then began to awkwardly shimmy the formfitting fabric over her hips.

"Here, let me do it," he said, his voice sounding as though he'd just swallowed gravel.

He grabbed the waistband, his warm fingers grazing her skin as he quickly and efficiently peeled the material down her legs and off her feet, then dropped the pants to the floor, leaving her in her camisole and black lace panties.

Derek stood at the edge of the bed, staring at what he'd revealed, and everything went still and quiet. A heated, lust-filled look crossed his features and darkened his gaze. His chest rose and fell rapidly as his breathing escalated, and the outline of his cock pressed insistently against the front of his pants.

He was undeniably hungry for her yet she could see him waging an internal battle, and she spoke up before he tried to leave again.

"*Derek,*" she breathed, the one word a desperate plea.

He gave his head a shake, as if yanking himself out of a trance. "I need to go," he said, and she heard the agonized indecision in his tone.

Now that she was no longer pretending to be intoxicated, she felt much too vulnerable in that moment—half-naked in front of him—but she pushed through her sudden nerves anyway. "Don't go. Stay. Please."

That same agony reached his eyes. "But you're drunk—"

"I'm not," she blurted out, needing him to know she was completely sober. "Not even a little bit. I had two drinks early on and the rest were nonalcoholic. I swear."

His head cocked to the side as realization dawned. "Wait, so all this was . . . an act?"

She bit her bottom lip and nodded.

He didn't seem angry or upset, thank God. In typical Derek fashion, at least with her, he appeared surprisingly amused that she'd gotten the better of him, and his lips quirked up.

She gave a little shrug from where she lay on the bed. "You were being so uptight, and I was just having some fun with you."

The tension visibly left his body, his shoulders dropping, his expression changing to one of pure desire. "Do you realize what you put me through tonight?"

"Me?" she said, feigning innocence.

"Yes, *you*," he replied and circled his fingers around one of her bare ankles, his thumb drawing slow, sweeping circles across her shin. "And you did it all *deliberately*."

"I did," she admitted, feeling herself melt

with every caress of his thumb. She swallowed hard, then added, "And now . . . I want you."

She'd just taken a huge risk putting her desires out in the open, but what Derek did next was not at all what she'd expected.

Chapter Thirteen

Jessica watched a slow, wicked smile spread across Derek's lips as he slid his hands up her legs, grabbing her calves, and flipping her onto her stomach. She let out a startled squeak, but before she could react, he was up on the bed, straddling her thighs from behind, and his hand smacked her ass.

She sucked in a breath as heat bloomed across her butt cheek and found its way to the aching flesh between her legs. Beyond shocked, she pushed up on her elbows and glanced over her shoulder at him, and the look of pure, unadulterated sin on his face made her entire body jolt with desire.

"What was that for?" she asked, her voice breathless.

"For being so fucking naughty all night long." He spanked her again, twice more, until her skin felt like it was on fire . . . in a shockingly arousing way.

She dropped her head to the comforter, a moan unraveling from her throat. Her heart was racing, her nipples were painfully hard, and she wanted . . . more. "I really was a bad girl," she whispered.

He chuckled huskily. "Oh, you really were, sweetheart," he agreed, and followed that up with two more swats that had her shaking beneath him and her pussy pulsing with need.

He massaged her stinging bottom with both hands, his thumbs slipping beneath the elastic band of her panties, and followed that bit of lace down between her thighs until he was *so close* to touching her sex. She gripped the covers, and if it wasn't for him still straddling her thighs, she would have shamelessly spread her legs wide to give him all the access he wanted.

Arching her back, which also lifted her ass,

she whimpered helplessly, desperately. "Derek, please. . ."

He removed his palms from her bottom and planted them on either side of her arms, leaning over her from behind. His body was warm and firm along hers, powerful and masculine as he pressed her into the mattress. He was still wearing his pants, but the thick length of his erection nudged against her backside, and all she could think about was finally having all those inches deep inside her.

"You've been yanking my chain all evening, so now *this* is how things are going to go. For the rest of the night, I'm going to be calling the shots. Got it?" he asked, his voice rough in her ear.

This dominant, sexually aggressive side to him was thrilling, and she didn't hesitate with her answer. "Yes."

He sat back up, moving her hair to one side and trailing his fingers down her bare back, tracing the crisscross of her camisole's straps, until he reached the point where it tied together at her lower back. He gave the strings a pull, the ties unraveled, and that easily the camisole pooled on the bed beneath her chest.

A low, rumbling sound erupted from his throat. "Jesus, one little tug and that's all it took for this top to fall off?"

His incredulous tone made her bite back a smile. "Yes."

"That could have happened in the goddamn club," he growled. "I ought to spank you a few more times for that alone."

Yes, please. She braced herself for the swat, but instead he gripped his fingers into the waistband of her panties and drew them down her legs as he moved off her body. When he was standing by the side of the bed, he untangled her undies from her feet and dropped them to the floor, leaving her completely naked.

"Turn over, Jessica," he ordered in a soft yet firm tone.

She closed her eyes for a moment, refusing to let any of those old insecurities get the best of her. Normally, she wasn't so self-conscious, but he wasn't a random stranger looking to get laid for the night or someone she'd never see again. This was Derek, a man she'd known and wanted for most of her life . . .and a man, she told herself, who wouldn't be in her bedroom if he truly didn't want *her*.

That reminder chased away three-quarters of her uncertainties. The other twenty-five percent still caused her to feel vulnerable, but she exhaled a deep breath and rolled to her back, anyway. Her hands instinctively covered her breasts, and she angled one knee in one of those alluring poses she'd been taught flattered her figure.

Derek had already unbuttoned his shirt, and he shrugged it off, revealing his toned and muscular upper body. His gaze slid over her and he tipped his head and arched a brow. "Put your hands down and open your legs," he murmured in a tone that was both coaxing and unyielding. "No modesty between us. I want to see all of you."

She couldn't quite bring herself to follow his order. "I know I'm not your usual type—"

"Let me make something clear." He cut her off, almost angrily. "You *are* my type, or else I wouldn't be standing in front of you with my cock so damn hard I could fucking pound nails. Everything about you is beautiful and desirable and I want to see what's mine." The last part of his sentence came out as a demanding growl

179

that sent shivers down her spine and bolstered her courage.

*Well, alrighty then . . .*She dropped her hands to her sides and let her knees fall open, shedding every last bit of inhibition for the night.

His jaw clenched as his dark eyes traveled up her legs, over her exposed and throbbing pussy, along her soft stomach and the swell of her hips, to her large, heavy breasts and the aching nipples that seemed to grow tighter under his hungry gaze.

"You're fucking perfect," he said, his eyes finally meeting hers as he started unfastening his pants. "Don't ever hide any part of your body from me. Understand?"

And that was that. "Yes, sir."

He smirked. "You're learning."

She watched as the rest of his clothes came off, enjoying the strip show. Once he was naked, he fisted his erection and moved toward the bed.

Suddenly he stopped and swore beneath his breath. "I don't have any condoms with me," he said, clearly not happy about the realization. "I'm clean, but I don't want to risk—"

"It's fine . . . *I'm* fine. And I'm on birth control." Because it helped some of her PCOS symptoms. And the thought of him sliding into her, without anything separating their bodies, was too much of a treat to miss.

"Good." With that settled, he moved up onto the bed, pushing her knees wide apart and trailing damp kisses along her inner thigh, building her anticipation. Finally, he reached the apex of her thighs and she squirmed, dying to feel his mouth on her sex.

"First things first," he murmured, placing her legs over his shoulders. His hands held her hips and his warm breath cascaded over her sex. "These gorgeous thighs . . . I want them wrapped around my face and shaking as I eat your pussy."

His dirty words shot liquid lust through her veins, and the stroke of his tongue licking up her seam had her clutching the comforter and arching her back. She exhaled a gasping breath, then groaned as he did exactly what he'd promised and devoured her like no man ever had before. Like he was starved and she was his feast.

His mouth was relentless, his bold licks

making her dizzy and desperate, and the graze of his teeth against her ultrasensitive flesh sent her reeling. He sucked on her clit, fucked her with his tongue, then went back to teasing that bundle of nerves with long, slow swirls that had her sobbing for relief.

The pressure and need inside her grew, and she would have thrashed on the bed had he not pinned her hips down with his fingers, which were sure to leave marks on her skin. When she was at the pinnacle of detonating, at the point of begging—and yes, her legs were shaking—he finally tipped her over the edge.

With a hoarse cry of pleasure, she came in quick, fluttering pulses against his tongue, her legs tightening against his head as she gave herself over to the most intense, earth-shattering orgasm of her life. Finally, her breathing evened and her heartbeat slowed, *and God*, she hoped there were more where that came from. She'd take all she could hoard this weekend because those kinds of orgasms were potentially addicting and this time with him was all she had.

His lips drifted across her stomach, and she opened her eyes, glancing down to find a very smug look on Derek's face, his own gaze still hazy with lust. He slowly kissed his way upward and pushed her thighs wider apart for him to settle between.

"Much better than any battery-operated boyfriend, huh?" he teased.

She huffed out a laugh. "I don't know . . . we still have that outstanding question about your stamina."

He reached her breasts and pushed them together before running his tongue around her areolas. Then, he plucked her nipples with his fingers until they hurt so good and she was squirming beneath him again.

"Oh, I've got staying power, sweetheart, so I don't want to hear any complaints when you're up all night riding my cock. I swear you'll be exhausted in the morning."

"Promises, promises," she said, then yelped when he sucked hard on a nipple, releasing it with a pop of sound, and grinned at her.

But the playful banter dissipated a moment later when he finally had their bodies aligned perfectly—his face right above hers, her thighs bracketing his hips, and the head of his cock nudging at her core.

"Ready for round two?" he asked, rocking another inch inside her, teasing her with the promise of being stretched and filled.

"You can certainly try," she replied, and yes, she was provoking him. She rarely had one orgasm with a man, let alone two, but Derek was already proving to be the exception.

"Mmm, I love a good challenge," he murmured as he buried his hands in her hair and let his lower body sink deeper and deeper into hers, drawing out the anticipation and delicious pleasure one hard, torturous inch at a time.

His gaze was on her the entire time, watching as her lips parted on soft gasps as he stroked along nerve endings she hadn't known existed, the way her lashes fluttered when she thought she couldn't take much more, and how her eyes rolled back in pure bliss when he was finally buried to the hilt.

He dipped his head against her neck and shuddered. "So damn good," he groaned, then started to move—slow, deep, endless strokes of his cock that had her melting with pleasure.

He kissed and nipped her throat, biting that sensitive spot where her neck and shoulder met, then sucked on a patch of skin that had sensation spiraling down to her clit. She inhaled a startled breath when that spark turned into a flash of need, the friction from his cock causing renewed chaos where she didn't think she had anything left.

With a soft moan, she grabbed on to his back and dragged her nails down his spine, wrapping her legs tight around his waist as her second orgasm crashed through her. She cried out his name, her pussy clenching and unclenching around his cock, and the growl that rumbled in his chest vibrated through her entire body, making her toes curl as she rode out the ecstasy.

He lifted his head, locking his eyes on hers, watching and making sure she finished before he allowed himself to lose control. His breathing grew harsh, his driving strokes becoming more erratic as he lunged harder, deeper into her pussy, until his own body tensed as he climaxed. The muscles in his back bunched against her fingertips as he shuttled into her one last time and came long, hard, and deep.

He breathed heavily on top of her and she

closed her eyes, sifting her fingers through his hair as they both attempted to gain their bearings. She especially needed a moment to process what had just happened—and tried her best to keep things in perspective, making sure her mind didn't spiral into girlish fantasies that couldn't come true.

As for her heart, it was already too late.

Jessica woke up the following morning with a content, blissful smile on her face—and the space next to her on her bed disappointingly empty. With a sigh, she smoothed her palm over the cool sheets, then gathered the pillow into her arms and inhaled the scent that Derek had left behind. Warm. Musky. Masculine.

She closed her eyes as delicious, decadent memories flooded her mind, the kind that true fantasies were made of. Except now, after last night with Derek, all those sexy dreams had become reality and had exceeded anything her imagination had ever conjured up. She'd never known that sex could be so good and satisfying, and since she was certain no other man would ever live up to Derek's level of expertise, at least she had those memories for the future, when he was gone.

Noises from the kitchen drifted up to her room, and soon after, the enticing aroma of coffee lured her from her warm bed. She took a quick shower, brushed her teeth, then put on a silk robe and headed down to the kitchen.

She found Derek standing at the counter, chopping vegetables and the ham she'd had in the refrigerator. He also had out a carton of eggs, grated cheese, and the bagels she'd bought last week. He was wearing running shorts, a tank T-shirt, and his hair was a rumpled mess on his head.

"Morning," she said as he finished dicing the meat and vegetables. While he washed his hands, she headed straight for the pot of coffee.

He walked toward her as she poured the brew into the mug he'd set out for her, making her heart flutter inside her chest as she watched him approach, then stop in front of her with a warm smile.

"Morning, beautiful," he murmured, then took her off guard as he dipped his head, placing a lingering kiss on her lips before gently rubbing his soft stubble against her cheek.

The gesture was so intimate it made her breath catch and her body melt. She hadn't been expecting such an affectionate morning after greeting, not that she was complaining, because Derek *did* make her feel beautiful, in every way.

He pulled back to look into her eyes as he tenderly brushed back a few stray strands of hair that had escaped the knot on her head. "You're just in time for me to make you an omelet. How are you feeling this morning?"

"Exhausted, in the very best way," she admitted, and blushed as she recalled the many times and many different ways Derek had fucked her. "And sore in all the right places."

He chuckled, the sound low and sexy. "Then I did my job well. That should teach you to question a man's stamina. Especially mine."

His playful demeanor made her smile. "Duly noted."

He moved away to pop two bagels into the toaster and then melt a pat of butter in a frying pan on the stove. "Finish making your coffee. Breakfast will be ready in a few minutes."

She wanted to say she could get used to this kind of routine—being spoiled and greeted in the morning with soft kisses and touches—but that implied more than one night together, and she knew better than to make any assumptions. Last night had been beyond fantastic, but it didn't equate to a relationship or commitment of any sort.

She stirred cream and sugar into her coffee, then leaned against the counter and took a sip of the caffeinated brew. "How long have you been awake?" she asked, noting it was after nine in the morning.

"A while," he said, pouring the eggs into the pan to start the first omelet, and while the mixture set up, he glanced her way. "I went out for a jog and finished up a few final things on your to-do list, so those items are pretty much done. By the way, I love your neighborhood. It's so quiet and friendly and quaint."

"I know," she agreed. "I love it here. New York City is full of life and excitement twenty-four seven, but there's something to be said for living somewhere simple and peaceful." She took another drink of her coffee. "At the end of the day, after working in the city at Curvy Girl, this is where I want to be. Someplace where I can relax and unwind and not hear fire engines at all hours of the day and night. Or be able to go out to eat at a family-owned restaurant that doesn't take months to get a reservation."

He laughed as he filled the omelet with veggies, meat, and cheese, then flipped it in half like he'd made a hundred of them before. "I can definitely see why you find it all so appealing."

She tipped her head curiously. "Have you ever thought about moving out of the city?"

He shook his head and plated the first omelet, then started on a second one. "No. I never had any reason to. And I just bought a new penthouse that's close to the office. Within walking distance, actually, so I'm not sure it would make sense to buy a place in the suburbs. At least, not until I get married and have a family. I definitely want my kids to grow up in a house instead of being cooped up in an apartment, so they have a yard and can play outdoors with their friends or ride their bikes to the park."

Jessica couldn't ignore the pang of melancholy she felt as he talked about marriage and having a family and kids. The one area in which she would always feel inadequate because she had no idea what the future held for her or what her body was capable of in terms of having children. But this conversation wasn't about *them*, and so she could only listen to how Derek envisioned his own future to be— without her.

They ate breakfast, and when they were through and Derek insisted on cleaning up the kitchen one last time, Jessica went back upstairs to change into a blouse and a pair of jean capris for the day. After brushing out her hair and applying a light amount of makeup, she left her room, hearing the water running in the guest bathroom across the hall.

Her body warmed all over as she envisioned Derek taking a shower and wondered what would happen if she made the spontaneous, and bold, decision to join him. She debated, but in the end, she didn't follow through with the idea. With last night over, in the light of day, she didn't want to be presumptuous about anything when it came to the two of them.

So, she went downstairs to her office and pulled up the illustrator program on her laptop computer. She scanned in the drawing she'd sketched Friday night so that she could put the finishing touches on the design and then move on to the pattern process before she selected fabrics for manufacturing.

A short while later, Derek came into the room, his hair damp, his face freshly shaven, dressed in a pair of jeans and a T-shirt. He set the duffle bag he'd packed and brought for the weekend onto the floor, then strolled over to the drafting table where she was working.

He was clearly ready to go and her stomach twisted in disappointment.

He smiled at her. "I'm pretty sure I finished everything around the house that was on your list, but if not, just let me know and I'll find the time to come back and get it done."

She slid off her chair so that she was standing, doing her best to hide the sadness filling her now that their time together was at an end. "So . . . I guess I should thank you for this weekend."

He arched a dark brow. "You mean the work around the house, right?"

She nodded, her cheeks flushing. "Yes . . . and well, everything else." Including sex, though she didn't outright say the word.

"Jessica," he said, his voice a slow, deep growl, "I didn't sleep with you because you paid for me at the auction. For Christ's sake, I'm not a prostitute."

She rolled her eyes at him, trying to keep things light. "I didn't mean it like that but I'm aware last night was just a one-time thing. And since it was fun and hot and sexy . . . it deserves to be included in that thank you."

He paused for a moment, his intense green eyes holding hers. "What if I want it to be more than a one-time thing?"

Her heart nearly stopped in her chest, then resumed beating at a rapid pace as she tried to process his unexpected question. What, exactly, was he suggesting? Did he want them to be friends with benefits? Was he looking for a random hookup when the urge struck? An occasional fling? She needed him to spell out what he wanted.

"What do you mean?" she asked in a cautious tone.

He leaned against the drafting table and

crossed his arms over his chest. "Would you go to my father's political fundraiser event with me next weekend?"

Surprise trickled through her. "Like, as your date?" she asked, unable to keep the skepticism from her voice.

"Yes, *my date*," he clarified with a sexy half grin. "These political events are so fucking trite and stuffy, and I could really use a plus-one so I'm not bored to tears." Reaching out, he skimmed his fingers along her jaw, then down the side of her neck, making her shiver from his touch. "And if we end the night in my bed, that would just be icing on the cake."

He wasn't offering her anything more than being his date at a social event. No promises, no commitment—not that she expected more when he'd already addressed his concerns about her brother being his best friend and business partner.

What he was proposing was casual, and she took the invitation at face value. Two people enjoying each other's company, and if sex happened, all the better. Considering how much she had on her plate with the Curvy Girl Couture Lingerie launch coming up and the

Belle Demoiselle contract within reach, she had enough to juggle without overthinking things with Derek. So, she decided that she'd just enjoy her time with him, for as long as it lasted, and not read too much into a few outings together here and there.

He was waiting for her response, and she gave him a genuine smile. "Sure, I'll go with you."

"Good." He looked oddly relieved, as if he hadn't been certain what she'd say. "I'll send an email to the event coordinator and have you added as my guest. I have a really busy week at the office, but I'll be in touch about the details."

"Okay. . . I guess I'll see you then."

"You will," he replied with one of those playful grins, then slid his hand around to the back of her neck, dipped his head toward hers, and captured her mouth with his.

A soft, surprised sound escaped her parted lips, giving him the perfect opportunity to deepen the connection. And he did. This kiss was nothing like the chaste one he'd treated her to in the kitchen earlier. His tongue swept inside, curling and tangling seductively around hers, lighting her up, and immediately kindling a desire that made her want to rip his clothes off and have her way with him right there on the floor of her office.

By the time he ended the kiss and stepped back, she was breathless, overwhelmed, and *aching*. And when he looked down at her, the barely there smirk that appeared on his lips told her that it had all been a deliberate ploy on his part, the rogue.

"I just wanted to give you something to think about and look forward to," he said, his own voice deep and husky as he gave her a sexy wink, then grabbed his duffle bag and headed toward the front door.

She watched him go, not sure how she was going to wait an entire week until she saw him again.

Chapter Fourteen

Armed with a Caffè Americano and all the caffeine his body could handle, Derek headed into Blackout Media early on Monday morning before the receptionist, the other employees, or his partner arrived. After taking the weekend off from work to give Jessica his undivided attention—which she deserved after paying a jaw-dropping amount for him at the auction— he knew he needed to get a jump-start on the week ahead.

He and Ben had made the decision to move forward on the buyout of MegaReelz, and it was full speed ahead. Contracts were being drawn up, they had various meetings with their lawyers to attend, and one of their teams had already come up with a business plan to present to him and Ben that included a marketing strategy, competitor analysis, and financial projections.

It was the most exciting and exhausting part of acquiring a new company. Exciting because of the potential growth and profitability of taking a struggling streaming platform and elevating it to the next level, and exhausting because of all the time involved in making that success happen. There were a lot of moving parts until everything was fully integrated.

A knock on his door a while later made him glance up from his laptop screen to see Ben strolling into his office. He was wearing a navy-blue business suit for the meeting with their attorneys today, but it was clear by the bemused expression on his face that he wasn't there to discuss their latest acquisition.

"I just wanted to see for myself that you survived the weekend with my sister," Ben said, humor in his voice as he released the button on his jacket, then sat down in one of the chairs in front of Derek's desk.

"I did," he replied, thinking back to the rocky start they'd had and how it eventually ended, with him wanting to see where things could go between them beyond the weekend. "After you left on Friday, we came to an understanding, and yes, that meant me doing all the work around her house to make up for that summer she was grounded because of my big mouth."

Ben chuckled. "Knowing Jessica, I bet she had a great time bossing you around."

Remembering how she'd driven him crazy with that sassy attitude for most of Saturday afternoon, Derek grinned. "Oh, yeah, she did."

"So, everything good between you two, then?" he asked. "Neither of you killed the other, so I'll take that as a good sign."

Even though the question was asked casually, humorously even, Derek felt like Ben was looking for reassurance that everything was okay, considering the last time he'd seen them together his sister had been pissed off at Derek for hiring contractors.

Ben's phone rang and he looked at the screen. "Hold that thought," he said to Derek and rose, stepping toward the side of the room to have a conversation with whoever was on the other line, giving Derek the opportunity to think through his reply.

It would be easy enough to tell Ben, *Jessica and I are fine* and let it go at that. But he had a lot of respect for his friend and partner, and Derek wasn't about to hide the fact that he planned to date Jessica—even if Jessica herself seemed skeptical about his intentions.

He'd seen the doubt in her eyes yesterday when he'd asked her to accompany him to his father's fundraiser event. And she'd questioned whether or not he wanted to openly date her—though he was pretty sure she just considered this an extension of their little hookup. Which was fine, for now. Until he had the chance to prove to her that their connection was about so much more than just sex.

And with Jessica's past and latent insecurities, that would take time and patience, and he was willing to put in the work. She was used to her own mother belittling her, and men who made her feel as though she wasn't good enough. Though she presented herself with confidence in most situations, he'd discovered there was still enough of that vulnerable girl inside of her to make her doubt her own worth.

The weekend with her had been an eye-opening experience. He'd spent the past few years keeping his attraction to her under wraps, but their forced proximity had revealed many intriguing facets to Jessica. He'd witnessed a joyful side to her personality, a sexy side, and a vulnerable one. She was smart and funny. Ambitious and creative. Not to mention, kind, caring, and honest—three attributes he'd learned to truly appreciate after everything he'd gone through with Claire.

If not for this weekend, he never would have known just how well they fit together. That this woman he'd practically grown up with because of his friendship with her brother was Derek's ideal woman in so many ways. And now that he knew how much he wanted her in his life, he had to admit his intentions to Ben.

As if on cue, Ben ended his call and stepped back toward Derek's desk. "Sorry about that. One of the lawyers needed me to clarify something."

Derek nodded, then got right to the point.

"You asked about me and Jessica and there's something I need to tell you."

Ben's brows furrowed, his suspicion clear. "Which is?"

Derek sat up straight in his chair, folded his hands on his desk, and looked his best friend right in the eyes. "I'm interested in your sister and I want to date her." Ben's eyes opened wide, and before he could reply, Derek went on. "I invited her to my father's fundraiser this weekend. She agreed and I wanted you to hear about the two of us from me. Because as much as I respect our friendship and our partnership, I need to see where this thing with your sister goes."

Ben remained quiet, that frown still in place, and Derek braced himself for a fight. After all, that had been his impulse when he'd first found out about Asher and *his* sister.

Ben rubbed a hand along his jaw and gave Derek a long, assessing look. "I have to admit, I didn't see this coming. At least on your end. I mean, I know Jessica has always had a crush on you, but ... this is still a surprise." His reasonable tone told Derek that his friend would be more rational than he'd been.

"So ... you don't want to hit me?" He'd been braced for anything.

Ben shook his head and let out a low chuckle. "No. Because I *know* you, and you're the kind of guy I'd want for my sister."

"Thank you," he said, a rush of relief draining the tension from his body.

Ben held up one hand. "However, it goes without saying that if you do something stupid and hurt her, then we're going to have a problem. I'd put my sister before the business. Before our friendship. I need you to know that."

"I would never hurt her," he assured Ben.

There were no guarantees in any relationship, but for Derek, this wasn't a short-term affair and Jessica wasn't just a fling. He saw a potential future with her, and he was willing to do anything in order to prove his feelings went beyond the friendship that had always existed between them. She meant more to him than he was able to put into words.

"Then we're good." Ben glanced at the time on his cellphone. "We've got a meeting with the lawyers in twenty minutes, so I'll let you finish up whatever you were doing and I'll see you in the conference room."

Ben strode out the door and Derek let out a long sigh of relief. That had gone way better than he'd anticipated and he was able to return his attention to his laptop to finish reading through the document before their meeting started.

A few minutes later his cell phone rang, and he glanced over to see his mother's name on the display. He tried to tamp down his annoyance because he *knew* why she was calling him so early in the morning. He'd bet every penny he had in the bank she'd already heard about the email he'd sent to the event coordinator for his father's fundraiser, requesting Jessica be added as his guest, and she wasn't happy. Collette Bettencourt kept her fingers in every aspect of her husband's campaign activities and would have been notified of the change immediately.

Jesus Christ, his snobby, social, and political climbing mother was so fucking predictable. Refusing to deal with her complaints and criticism, he let the call go to voicemail. Once he received an alert the call had ended, he listened to the message she'd left for him . . . about how she'd gotten a call from the event coordinator and he rolled his eyes as she droned on.

"How could you bring a date?" his mother ranted in a high-pitched tone. "Are you trying to be cruel and make Claire jealous? She's going to be there all alone. Did you even think about how awkward and embarrassing that's going to be for her, you bringing another woman when it should be *her* on your arm?"

"Are you fucking kidding me?" He'd heard enough and slammed his finger down on the screen, ending and deleting the voicemail. His mother was dense and irrational and he was finished listening to her delusions of how his life should go.

He typed out a reply text: *I'm a grown man who can make his own decisions, and I'm bringing Jessica. Claire will get over it because we are no longer a couple and I owe her nothing. If it's an issue for her, then that's her problem, not mine. Not up for discussion.*

He sent the message, and within a minute, his phone rang again. Another call from his mother that he ignored, and she left yet another voicemail he didn't bother listening to.

There was no point. Nothing she could say or do would change his mind about the classy, beautiful woman he intended to have on his arm for the night.

* * *

Would you rather receive a sexy photo or a sexy phone call?

Jessica read the text from Derek and grinned as she headed back to the boutique with Avery. They'd had a successful lunch meeting with Belle Demoiselle and he'd left his message for her while she'd been busy. She'd been receiving random flirtatious and suggestive texts since they'd parted ways on Sunday. Now, it was Thursday, and she had to admit that she was enjoying his playful, sexy *which would you rather* game.

The getting-to-know-her questions came sporadically throughout the day and evening. He'd started with light, neutral queries that had graduated into more intimate, provocative inquiries. She never knew what he'd ask, but whenever her phone chimed with a message from Derek, butterflies erupted in her stomach and a perma-grin lifted her lips.

Considering both their schedules were so busy, it was a fun and unexpected way for him to stay in touch. She also loved knowing he was thinking about her, despite them being apart.

She typed back, *Well, I've never done either, but since there are a dozen ways things could go wrong by sending a sexy photo, I think I'd rather have a sexy phone call.*

I knew you liked my dirty talk, he returned and added a smirking emoji.

She felt her cheeks warm and quickly responded, *I do.*

Naughty girl. I have a dinner meeting and should be home by nine thirty. Be in bed, wearing your sexiest lingerie, and I'll FaceTime you at ten for that sexy phone call.

"You're grinning again. And blushing," Avery pointed out in a lighthearted tone as they walked along the sidewalk toward the Curvy Girl Couture boutique. "I take it you're answering Derek's naughty questions?" She wriggled her brows as she asked.

"Yes," she said, feeling giddy inside. "We have a FaceTime date tonight."

"Oooh. That sounds fun."

Jessica laughed, already feeling the anticipation build. "I'm sure it will be."

Avery smiled at her. "I like seeing you happy."

"I'm always happy," she said automatically.

Her friend looped her arm through Jessica's. "I like seeing you happy *with a man*," she clarified. "It's about damn time someone appreciated *everything* about you."

"Derek and I aren't like that," Jessica refuted, trying to stay sensible and realistic about her affair with him. "It's just a fun fling. And I'm happy in general right now. Life is good, and today's lunch meeting with Audrey and her partner couldn't have gone any better."

"I agree." Excitement filled Avery's voice. "You are *this* close to getting your own exclusive lingerie line." She pinched her fingers close together for emphasis.

Jessica's elation was nearly overwhelming, but she wasn't one to tempt fate by assuming anything. Nothing was guaranteed until a contract was signed. But after today's lunch with Audrey and Gisele, she agreed she was one step closer to making that dream come true.

They'd asked to see a few more sketches and new ideas, and she'd shown them the ensemble she'd drawn over the weekend, which they both gushed over. Jessica knew they were waiting to see how the launch of Curvy Girl Couture Lingerie went and how well the line was received by influencers and celebrities. They'd gauge the response from the editors of fashion magazines like *Allure, Elle, Marie Claire*, and *Glamour*, as well.

Jessica had a lot of key industry people to impress, and while she believed in her designs, and Audrey and Gisele seemed to love her concepts, the promise of an offer could easily be revoked for any reason, and that possibility was always in the back of her mind.

They arrived at the boutique and strolled inside. They'd only been gone for a little over an hour, but Maddie was juggling three customers and appeared a bit frazzled trying to accommodate each woman.

"Oh, good, you're back." Relief spilled from her voice as she hung a few outfits over her arm that the woman beside her wanted to try on.

"Jessica, a friend stopped by to see you and insisted on staying until you returned from lunch. I told her she could wait in the back lounge."

Jessica blinked in surprise. She had no appointments for the afternoon, and no friends had called or messaged to say her they'd be stopping by. "Who is it?"

"Her name is Claire," Maddie said as she escorted the customer to the dressing room. "I was going to text you to let you know, but I've had my hands full."

Shock jolted through Jessica along with concern. What could that woman want?

"Did I do anything wrong?" Maddie asked.

"Of course not!" She wasn't angry at Maddie for letting Claire stay.

Maddie had only been an employee and friend for a little over a year. She didn't know Jessica's history with Claire. But Avery did and when Jessica turned, her friend's expression was full of fury. They both knew Claire wasn't there to extend an olive branch or to indulge in any kind of pleasant conversation.

"No worries," Jessica assured Maddie,

keeping her tone low and sweet since there were customers in the store.

Avery, meanwhile, looked ready to charge into the back room, guns blazing on her behalf. As much as she appreciated her friend's support, Jessica knew that wouldn't go over well. Besides, she wasn't afraid to deal with Claire on her own.

She smiled at Avery, keeping up the *everything's fine* pretense. "Why don't you help Maddie with these women, and I'll go see what Claire wants."

Avery's brows furrowed into a frown. "Are you sure?"

Jessica nodded, her earlier good mood already evaporating. "I'll be fine."

Exhaling a deep breath, Jessica headed to the back of the store, then through the curtained doorway that led to a large, open room sectioned off with various areas. Jessica had her office, a store room, a lounge with a sofa, a small table to eat a meal, and a work area —where Claire was currently looking through the dozens of photo proofs that Jessica had been sorting through earlier that morning from the previous week's lingerie shoot.

She'd already selected the best shots for the catalog for the launch party and sent them off for final editing and retouching where needed. But the fact that Claire had invaded her private space and was going through the photos as if she had every right enraged Jessica.

Claire was so engrossed in the display of snapshots that she hadn't heard Jessica enter, but as soon as she picked up one of the pictures, Jessica saw red and snapped.

"What are you doing here?" she demanded.

Startled, Claire jumped, dropped the photo, and spun around, her hand grasping the small Chanel cross-body purse at her hip. She knew she'd been caught snooping, but her surprised expression quickly schooled into a cool, composed look.

"I hope you're not planning on using any of these pictures for anything important. I've heard talk and speculation in the fashion industry Belle Demoiselle is interested in your line of lingerie for *chubby* girls, and these photos aren't very flattering."

Jessica's jaw clenched. She knew Claire wasn't referring to smoothing skin tones or adjusting the lighting on the shots, but rather she believed the curvy, voluptuous women themselves weren't beautiful. The bitch.

"There's no good reason I can think of for you to be in my store, so what do you want?" Jessica asked again.

"You're right about that. Nothing here appeals to me." Claire glanced at the rack of fashionable fall separates that were tagged and ready to go onto the floor and wrinkled her nose. "I just stopped by to tell you that I know you were at Club Ten29 with Derek on Saturday, grinding all over him on the dance floor."

Jessica rolled her eyes, not at all surprised that her minions, Peyton and Tiffany, had relayed that information. "Seriously, *that's* what you came here to say?"

"I also heard that you're going as Derek's guest to his father's fundraising event." Claire's lips pursed in annoyance.

"*And*?" Jessica prompted impatiently.

"Look, you paid for a weekend with him and had your fun." Claire's chin lifted haughtily. "Now, I just wanted to tell you in person that you really ought to end things with him before things end badly for *you*."

"Excuse me?" Jessica's tone rose a few octaves. "Is that a threat?"

A fake smile touched the corners of Claire's lips. "It's just a *friendly* warning, because I really don't want to see you get hurt."

Jessica huffed out a sarcastic laugh. "Yeah, I'm going to have to call bullshit on that one."

Anger flashed in Claire's eyes at Jessica's repeated ability to control the narrative of the conversation. "He'll get bored and realize that what we have together is much stronger than whatever he could possibly have with you."

"What you *had* together," Jessica corrected her, her emphasis on the past tense of the word stated very clearly.

"Oh, he'll come around," Claire shot back. "And at the very least, he's not going to stay satisfied with someone like you for very long. He's probably just extending things with you so you feel like you've gotten your money's worth."

Despite her outward show of bravado, Claire's taunt hit a sore spot and Jessica sucked in a pained breath. The dig was intentional and cruel, though not a surprise coming from someone who'd made bullying an art form.

Some very choice, unladylike words jumped to the tip of Jessica's tongue, but she kept her composure, refusing to stoop to Claire's level or justify her relationship with Derek when the other woman was deliberately provoking her just to get a reaction. One Jessica refused to give her.

She maintained her poise, but this time she had no comeback to offer. There was no denying that Claire's cruel words burrowed deep, poking at the last stubborn dregs of childhood insecurities—of not being good enough. Not for her mother or someone like Derek. Ironically it wasn't that she believed he'd ever go back to Claire, nor was it her voluptuous body that made her feel less than, something that would probably shock the mean woman standing in front of her.

It was Jessica's possible fertility issues that weighed on her soul. There was no doubt in her mind that Derek would want kids one day— he'd told her as much. That house, the yard to play outdoors, and the development where they could ride bikes to the park with friends. His own words. Moving on from a fling or relationship or whatever she labeled it was inevitable.

Jessica wanted to smack the triumphant smirk off of Claire's face but kept her hands to herself. "Get out of my store," she said with a shocking amount of calm. "And you're not welcome back unless you'd like to be arrested for trespassing."

"As if I'd ever *want* to come back," Claire scoffed, then marched around Jessica and out of the back room.

A few seconds later, Avery was by her side, looking furious on Jessica's behalf. "I heard most of that . . . she's such a bitch. Are you going to tell Derek?"

Jessica released a deep breath that did little to ease the tension in her chest and shook her head. "No."

"Why not?"

Moving to the table, Jessica busied herself with putting the photos Claire had been looking at into a folder. "Because it doesn't matter, and I'm not going to complain about his ex-fiancée bullying me." She rubbed her fingers across her forehead. "The last thing I want or need is him sticking up for me and causing potential issues between his parents and

Claire's parents, who are big political donors to his father's campaign."

Avery crossed her arms over her chest. "Don't you think that's for him to decide?"

"*I've* decided," she said, refusing to let Derek get in the middle of the issue. "I'm a grown woman. I can fight my own battles, and I just did."

The stiffness in Avery's posture softened, and she smiled. "Yeah, I'm proud of you. You definitely held your own with that catty bitch."

Unfortunately, Jessica didn't think it was going to be the last time she'd have to deal with the other woman. Not as long as Jessica was a part of Derek's life.

Chapter Fifteen

"**W**ould you rather have your hair pulled or your ass smacked?" Derek asked, casually spouting off yet another outrageous and lascivious question for her to answer.

Jessica nearly poked herself in the eye with the mascara wand she was using to coat the ends of her false lashes as Derek's deep, sexy voice drifted through the speaker on her phone. She should have been used to those random questions by now, but every time he asked one, her entire body tingled with awareness *everywhere*, which was probably his intent.

Currently, her nipples tightened against her silk robe at the thought of his fingers fisting in her hair and pulling her head back, and her stomach did a little somersault when she remembered how much she'd liked feeling the swat of his hand warming up her backside.

It had been a week since they'd slept together, and she couldn't deny she was anticipating an encore at the end of tonight. She might not have seen him in person during that time, but he was a master at building sexual tension with his dirty talk and husky voice in her ear, and she couldn't wait for the two of them to be alone. And for him to make good on all the information he'd gleaned with his *which would you rather* queries.

"Jesus, Derek," she said with a huff of laughter as she dropped her mascara back into her makeup bag and grabbed her blush, which at the moment she didn't need much of. "You can't be asking me these kinds of questions while I'm getting ready for the fundraiser gala tonight."

"Yes, I can, because I need to know your answer," he said, his voice sounding serious, despite the playful nature of this game that he seemed to enjoy as much as she did. "I want to prepare for *after* the fundraiser when I have you all to myself and stripped naked."

Stripped naked . . . that's how their Face-Time had gone Thursday night. He'd asked her to wear her sexiest lingerie, and she had, but he'd also demanded she take off each piece for him and touch herself in ways she'd only done on her own and in private—while he enjoyed the show. Once again, he'd obliterated her inhibitions while praising and coaxing her to a tsunami of an orgasm that left her dazed and breathless.

And then, he'd ordered her to *watch him*, and she hadn't been able to look away as he fisted his cock in his hand, stared into the phone's camera, and stroked himself off until he came all over his stomach. It had been one of the hottest things she'd ever seen or done, and she could still recall his erotic grunts and groans as he climaxed.

"You're thinking about Thursday night, aren't you?" he asked, a too-knowing smirk in his tone.

"I plead the Fifth." If she relived that night anymore, she was at risk of ruining her current pair of panties.

"Answer my question," he insisted.

As she considered the choices, she stared at her reflection in the bathroom mirror, her dramatic makeup nearly finished, except for lipstick, which she'd apply right before he arrived to pick her up. "I already know what it's like for you to smack my ass, so I'd have to go with pulling my hair."

"How about smacking your ass *while* pulling your hair?" he suggested.

She groaned. "You have to stop."

His chuckle was low and wicked. "One more. Would you rather have your hands tied during sex or wear a blindfold during sex?"

She plugged in her curling wand so she could get to work on her hair, which she'd decided to leave down tonight. "Is that all you think about?" she asked, smiling. "Sex?"

"With you? Yes," he replied. "It's been a week since I've had my hands on your body or my tongue in your pussy or my cock buried deep inside you while you come."

Her breath caught and her face flamed.

"So, hands tied during sex or a blindfold?" he went on, as if he hadn't just lit a torch to her body with those words.

"Which would *you* rather have me choose?" she asked, curious to know his preference.

"Hands tied," he replied without hesitating. "Which gives me all the control so I can fuck you any way I want while you beg me to let you come."

She groaned. "You're distracting me and I need to go, and don't you have to get ready for tonight, too?"

"I'm a guy," he said with a laugh. "I'm already showered, shaved, and just need to put on my tux."

"That's so not fair," she muttered and shook her head. "I'll see you soon, and keep your dirty *which would you rather* questions to yourself this evening and behave," she said with a chuckle in her voice.

"I make no promises."

Still smiling, she said goodbye. Jessica disconnected the call, then started curling her hair, a task that took her a good forty minutes because of the length. Yes, she could afford to hire a glam squad, but having a team of hair and beauty experts wasn't her thing. She knew what she liked, what worked best for her features, and she actually enjoyed the process of primping. She found it relaxing, which was what she needed to be before he arrived to pick her up.

She'd attended dozens of charity events and fundraisers over the years, and as comfortable as Derek made her feel, tonight's formal gala came with its own set of concerns, along with a bit of anxiety because Claire would be there. Jessica didn't think the other woman would say or do anything to make a scene—Claire preferred to show the hateful side of her personality in private while presenting herself as the height of decorum in social situations.

But this was her first outing with Derek, as a couple, and with his mother still pressuring him to give Claire another chance, Jessica knew there might be tension between them all. But she refused to let anyone see her anxiety or that she was anything other than confident in her relationship with Derek.

At five in the afternoon, Derek and his driver arrived to pick her up. It would take about an hour to get back to the city and to the hotel where the event was taking place. As soon as she opened the door, Derek's gaze took her in. His lips parted in awe, and his green eyes darkened as he gave her a slow, head-to-toe perusal. While he wore the same tailored tuxedo from the auction—and looked beyond handsome, like her own James Bond fantasy come to life—she'd chosen a newly designed gown from her own upcoming holiday collection, a slate-blue dress in a shimmering silk fabric that tastefully skimmed her curves and made her feel like a goddess.

"Holy . . . wow," he said huskily as he took her hand and placed a kiss on her knuckles. "You look absolutely stunning."

She smiled, warmed by the compliment and pleased with the desire in his gaze, which made the hours of primping worth it. "Thank you."

He exhaled what seemed like a tortured breath. "It's taking everything in me not to push you back inside your house and ravish you here and now. But I don't think you'd appreciate me smearing your lipstick, wrinkling your dress, or ruining your hair with my hands."

She laughed, trying to ignore the arousal already thrumming through her, just from his words alone. "No, but I appreciate the sentiment."

"Just know, later tonight, all bets are off." He gave her a hooded look and a small smirk. "This night can't be over fast enough."

She couldn't agree more, but Derek had an obligation to fulfill to his parents, and so off they went. She sat in the back of the Town Car with Derek, and their conversation was easy and effortless as they talked about his newest acquisition and Blackout Media's plans for MegaReelz. Then, he gave her his undivided attention as he asked about updates with her lingerie launch and the details of her lunch with Belle Demoiselle that week. His interest was genuine, and while Jessica always had Avery to talk to about business, having Derek listen and offer advice when asked was something she truly enjoyed and appreciated.

The time went by quickly, and soon their driver pulled up to the Four Seasons Hotel and came to a stop at the valet. An attendant opened her door, and Derek came around the car to join Jessica, then slipped his hand into hers as they entered the hotel together.

They made their way to the Greenwich

Ballroom, which was beautifully decorated for the occasion, with elaborate floral arrangements, lit candles, and an orchestra playing music. Waitstaff walked around with trays of champagne and hors d'oeuvres, while guests and donors for Derek's father's upcoming presidential campaign were already mingling.

They made the obligatory rounds during the cocktail hour, with Derek doing his part as senator Corbin Bettencourt's son, greeting people he knew in the political world, along with saying hello to family friends. Derek introduced Jessica to everyone he spoke to, keeping his hand in hers or his arm around her waist, clearly proud to have her by his side. While the men discussed business or politics, the women conversed with Jessica in a way that made her feel surprisingly accepted—probably because she was on the arm of a Bettencourt, but it didn't matter. Nobody treated her with anything other than politeness or respect.

Derek's father was busy glad-handing his loyal supporters, his wife and Derek's mother, Collette, by his side. And while Jessica had seen glimpses of Claire watching her with Derek, his ex-fiancée seemed content to remain with her own parents as they circled the room. As for Derek, he must have also been aware of Claire's whereabouts, because he managed to casually steer them in the opposite direction, for which Jessica was grateful.

At some point, they found their way to Derek's parents, and though Jessica remained outwardly relaxed and calm, inwardly she was guarded, unsure of what kind of reception she'd receive.

Derek shook his father's hand, gave his mother a light kiss on the cheek, then turned to Jessica with an encouraging *you got this* smile while slipping his hand back into hers. "Mom, Dad, you remember Ben's sister, Jessica?" he said by way of introduction.

"It's been some time, but yes, we do," Corbin said, his smile as kind and amiable as his tone. "It's a pleasure to have you here."

"Thank you, Senator Bettencourt," she replied.

"Please, call me Corbin," he insisted.

Turning her gaze, Jessica glanced at Collette, a beautiful woman who carried herself with poise and sophistication yet managed to emanate an aloof demeanor, the complete opposite of her husband's friendly disposition. Jessica wasn't sure if Collette's elitist attitude was a natural part of her personality or directed toward Jessica herself. After all, she already knew Collette wasn't happy with Derek's decision to date Jessica when she had other visions for her son's future.

Jessica remained composed and gave the other woman a gracious smile. "It's nice to see you, Mrs. Bettencourt. You look lovely tonight."

The other's woman's smile was tight-lipped. "Thank you."

That was it . . . no *please, call me Collette.* Or a polite *you look lovely as well.*

Derek gave her a hand a squeeze in a show of support and maybe even as an apology for Collette's rude behavior. It would have been nice to have his mother's acceptance, but Jessica wasn't surprised by the chilly reception, either.

"So, how's the latest acquisition coming along?" Corbin asked his son.

The two men launched into an easy discussion about business, and while it would have been normal for Collette to converse with Jessica, instead the other woman ignored her and glanced around the room, as if searching for someone more interesting to talk to. It was a blatant attempt to make Jessica feel insignificant and let her know she wasn't good enough for Derek, and she hated that this obnoxious woman had the ability to touch on those deep-seated insecurities.

Jessica did her best not to fidget and was grateful when she was saved by the announcement for everyone to take their seats for dinner. As soon as Derek led her in the direction of their assigned table, her shoulders lowered, her tense muscles loosened, and she was able to relax again.

"I'm so damn sorry about that," Derek said once they were out of earshot of his parents, his tone underscored with anger. "My mother can give the Ice Queen herself a run for her money, and I would have called her out on her bitchy attitude if we weren't in such a high-profile social setting."

"It's fine," she said, understanding that this wasn't the time or place for a family argument, though she appreciated his protectiveness. "Don't forget, I grew up with a mother just like yours, so I'm all too familiar with that kind of treatment."

His dark brows pulled together in a fierce frown. "Well, it's not okay. She seems to have gotten worse since Nikki ended their relationship."

Jessica sighed. "Ahh, that parental loss of control over their child. It drives them insane."

"I'm pretty sure my mother is feeling the same way about me and isn't sure what to do with the fact that both of her children have disappointed and defied her." His sensual lips turned downward, and she hated that his earlier good mood had changed because of his mother's behavior.

Jessica stopped him before they reached their table. Not caring who watched, she grasped the lapels of his tuxedo jacket, making sure she had his full attention before she spoke. "I don't want your mother to ruin what has been a very pleasant evening so far, so just take a deep breath and let it go so we can have fun for the rest of the night."

He exhaled long and hard, then slowly smiled at her, his anger gone. "Thank you. I needed that," he murmured, gratitude glittering in his gaze. He braced his hands on her hips, his fingers curling into her in an intimate, caring gesture.

"My pleasure." He deserved to be relaxed and happy.

"Sometimes I need reminding that my mother shouldn't have control over my emotions. Besides, I'd rather focus all my energy and attention on you."

Jessica loved the way that sounded. "Same here."

"Shall we?" He gestured forward and they found their table, then took their seats.

They spent an hour enjoying a delicious five-course meal and idle conversation with their dinner companions, followed by a speech from his father thanking everyone for coming and for their generous donations. He spoke about his presidential aspirations and the issues he intended to tackle should he decide to run for the highest office in the country. The speech ended with an obligatory standing ovation and segued into after-dinner dancing and a silent auction.

Unlike Club Ten29, where the music was deliberately loud, raucous, and invited a whole lot of dirty dancing, this band kept to the slower classics, and Jessica was pleasantly surprised when Derek led her out to the dance floor and pulled her into his embrace, their bodies aligning intimately. With one of his arms wrapped around her waist to keep her close and his other hand holding hers, they swayed to the music, their gazes locked, both of them smiling.

The warm, masculine scent of his cologne seduced her senses, and the feel of his hard thighs sliding against hers sparked a deeper need. There was nothing overtly sexual about their position—every other couple was dancing the same way—yet the closeness left her breathless and aroused.

His eyes darkened as they stared into hers, the blazing heat there sizzling across her skin. "So, I think my obligation here is done, and I'm ready to leave so I can have you all to myself."

She nodded much too eagerly and didn't care. "I just need to go to the ladies' room, and I'm all yours."

A searing look crossed his features at her words as he guided her off the dance floor. "I'll wait for you over by the entrance," he said, gesturing to the front of the ballroom.

She headed into the women's lounge, took care of business, and washed her hands, then she stepped out of the ladies' room and made her way to where Derek said he'd be waiting . . . except he wasn't alone. He stood with Claire, at least two feet separating them. His hands were shoved into the front pockets of his pants, his body language tense.

Jessica couldn't say she was surprised that his ex-fiancée had made a move on Derek when he was by himself, and she waited for her stomach to twist with the usual doubts and insecurities Claire brought about—but none came. Oddly enough, Jessica no longer felt threatened by her old nemesis because she trusted Derek completely.

Instead, annoyance filled her. She was tired of Claire and her continued persistence when she wasn't wanted. As Jessica made her way through the guests to Derek, she watched Claire's expressions—which ran the gamut from sly to seductive to irritation, then pleading. She couldn't hear their conversation yet, but Claire's changing features spoke volumes.

As did Derek's indifferent reaction to whatever she was saying.

As Jessica approached, Derek held up a hand, cutting Claire off. "I really don't know how to make this any clearer. We're done. I've moved on, and you need to do the same."

Jessica joined him and he automatically wrapped an arm around her waist, pulling her close. The gesture was both possessive and protective—not that she needed protecting from Claire—but for one of the few times in her life, she felt both wanted and secure.

Claire's mouth parted, her shock obvious before she schooled her features into a bland mask and raised her chin, her gaze narrowing on Jessica. "You'll never be good enough for him." She spoke in low tones, obviously not wanting anyone to overhear her lose control. "You might think you got your dream guy, the one you wrote about in your journals in high school, but there is no way it's going to last."

Jessica opened her mouth to tell the other woman to get over herself already, but Derek stiffened and spoke first.

"That's enough," he growled and immediately turned to Jessica. "Let's get the fuck out of here," he said, ignoring Claire completely.

"Sounds perfect," she said, putting a hand on his arm.

Claire glared one last time at Jessica, then spun around and walked away.

Jessica glanced at Derek. "Are you okay?"

As he looked at her, his gaze softened. "I'm fine but I'll be even better when we get home."

Chapter Sixteen

Settled into the back of the Town Car, Derek tried to calm his raging anger toward Claire—it was one thing for his ex to insult *him* after he'd rejected her advances for the umpteenth time since their breakup, but to turn her nastiness to Jessica was fucking unacceptable.

And what the hell had that been about, anyway? He'd seen Claire treat Jessica similarly at the bachelor auction. It was as though these two had a history of some sort—and a very antagonistic one on Claire's part. But he had no idea what the issue was.

He wanted to ask, but when he glanced over at Jessica and saw her looking out the back passenger window, subdued and with a pensive look on her face, he decided that those questions could wait. Claire had already put a damper on things, but Derek didn't want to ruin the rest of the evening. Tonight was about *them*, no outside influences to spoil a romantic evening that was still salvageable.

Derek didn't want to talk. He just wanted, no, *needed* Jessica.

He hit the privacy divider between the front and back seats, and Jessica turned her head, a surprised look on her face. She'd clearly been taking her cues from his bad mood, giving him space to deal with Claire's drama, but from this moment on, he wouldn't let his ex consume another second of his thoughts.

Focusing solely on Jessica, he gave her a wicked smile and crooked his finger at her. "Come sit on my lap."

She tipped her head to the side, a playfully coy look touching her expression. "Do you plan to take advantage of me in the back of this car, Mr. Bettencourt?"

"Possibly, Ms. Cavanaugh." He smirked, immersing himself completely in this seduction. "Why don't you come here and find out?"

Her teeth scraped across her bottom lip, and she looked hesitant for a moment. "Are . . . you okay? I mean, after all that?"

He warmed at her concern but there was no need for her to worry. "I'm here with you, so I'm better than okay." Then, he gave her a stern look and patted his lap. "Now come here."

His commanding tone did the trick. A flash of desire lit up her pretty eyes, and she slid across the leather bench seat, settling herself across his thighs. He slid a hand up her back, beneath the fall of her silky hair, then twisted his fingers in the strands close to the back of her scalp.

He gave it an experimental pull.

Her lips parted on a soft moan, and her lashes fell half-mast, telling him everything he needed to know: his sweet girl liked to be manhandled when it came to sex.

Keeping her hair fisted in his hand, he brought her mouth to his and kissed her. Slowly, thoroughly, deliberately—gradually deepening the connection and using his tongue to completely seduce her. Her body went lax against his, her palms sliding beneath his jacket and pressing against his chest as he continued to make out with her.

With his free hand, he pulled up the hem of her gown until the fabric reached her knees, then drew slow, languid circles up the inside of her thigh. She moaned into his mouth, and without him even having to ask, she spread her legs, inviting him even higher. He reached her panties, already damp with her arousal, and he pushed his fingers beneath the soaked panel of fabric to stroke her bare flesh.

She sucked in a quick breath, and he curled his tongue around hers, keeping her quiet as he filled her up with two of his fingers and pressed his thumb against her clit. Her legs fell open even wider, her hips rocking rhythmically against his hand as he lazily fucked her with his fingers and rubbed her clit.

He swallowed her moans and kept up his ministrations, bringing her to the edge of orgasm and stopping. She squirmed on his lap, whimpered against his lips, and tried to pull back her head to make other loud noises, but his fingers against her scalp controlled her movements.

Her hands gripped the front of his shirt as

he started up again, and when he finally lifted his mouth from hers so she could catch her breath, she looked at him with wild eyes, her cheeks beautifully flushed, her lips swollen from his long, ardent kisses.

"Derek, please," she begged, then shuddered when he dragged the pads of his fingers against that sweet spot inside of her.

"Please what, sweetheart?" he asked, curious to know if she'd say the actual words.

She bit her bottom lip, and when he flicked his thumb across her clit, her eyes nearly rolled back in her head. "Let me . . . make me come."

He tipped her head back even farther and skimmed his lips up along the side of her neck. "You're not ready yet."

"I'm beyond ready," she whispered, panting for breath. "You're teasing me."

He chuckled against her throat. "It's called edging, and by the time I let you orgasm, it's going to feel so fucking good and intense because of how much you want it. How much you *need* it."

He captured her mouth again in a series of deep, drugging kisses, sending her body on a roller coaster of highs and lows, again and again, until he finally felt the car slow as they exited the highway. Knowing they only had about five more minutes before they arrived at her house, he finally let her climax. He lifted his head to watch her face as she fell over the edge—a stunning sight that made his cock throb in the confines of his slacks.

She whimpered, trying to be quiet, while her pussy spasmed and clenched tight around his fingers and her entire body jerked with the last bit of pleasure coursing through her.

"So fucking beautiful," he murmured, removing his hand from beneath her dress, and while she watched, he sucked the taste of her from his fingers.

She exhaled a deep, shuddering breath, her eyes dark with desire. "God, the things you do to me."

He gave her a slow, sinful grin full of intent. "Oh, I'm just getting started tonight."

The Town Car pulled into Jessica's driveway, and Derek lifted her off his lap so he could open the back door, then helped her out. He let the driver know he was done for the night, then he grabbed Jessica's hand and promptly escorted her to the front door. Once

inside her house, he led her straight up to her
bedroom, because the only thing he could
think of was burying his cock inside her warm,
willing body.

He switched on the nightstand light so he
could see all of her. Anxious to feel her bare
skin, he quickly helped her out of her gown,
until she was standing in front of him, her full
breasts encased in a sexy beige satin and lace
bra and a pair of matching panties that was
sexy as fuck and made his dick ache.

He must have been staring at all her
gorgeous curves for longer than he'd realized,
because she moved toward him and started
tugging off his clothes with as much impatience
as he'd just exhibited. His jacket came first, and
while he yanked the bow tie around his neck
loose, she attacked the front of his shirt, nearly
ripping off the buttons in her haste to strip him
bare.

He kicked off his shoes, removed his socks,
and both of their hands collided at the belt
around his waist. She looked up at him with a
lust-filled gaze, then shook her head, causing all
that silky hair to cascade around her shoulders
and down to the swells of her luscious breasts.

"Let me," she said huskily, eagerly, and pushed his hand away.

He groaned. Who was he to refuse what the lady wanted? He let her take control of this one thing because he couldn't resist this uninhibited side to Jessica. Framing her face in his hands, he brought her mouth up to his, kissing her deep and dirty while she attempted to unbuckle his belt, her fingers faltering slightly because of the way he was distracting her.

She managed to open the front of his slacks, and her hand slid inside, stroking and squeezing along the length of his erection through the fabric of his boxer briefs. He growled against her mouth, and when she shoved his pants off his hips and they pooled around his feet, he kicked them off to the side.

He released her mouth, thinking of turning the tables, but she dropped her lips to his neck, trailing soft, damp kisses down to his chest, temporarily short-circuiting some of his brain cells when she grazed her teeth along his nipples. He could have stopped her . . . could have easily pushed her down on the bed and taken control, but her exploration felt too fucking good to end.

Her fingertips grazed along his abs, the muscles there flexing beneath her touch. Her mouth moved down his body, and he tipped his head back and groaned, his hands tangling in her hair as her silken breath made a path to his navel, then traversed lower. Her fingers gripped the waistband of his underwear, and she sank to her knees in front of him while stripping the briefs down his legs for him to step out of.

His stiff shaft jutted out right in front of her flushed face. She licked her lips and skimmed her palms up his thighs, then wrapped her fingers around his rigid length. The anticipation of what she'd do next made his cock pulse in her hand, and when she leaned forward and licked her tongue across the head, tasting the drop of fluid on the tip, there was no holding back the deep growl of need that erupted from his throat.

She glanced up at him with a coy smile, looking very pleased with his response, which seemed to embolden her even more. Her lush lips parted, surrounding his cock as she took every inch into her mouth, and her silky tongue stroked along the underside of his dick. With a hum of pleasure, she closed her eyes and began sucking his cock, slow and languidly at first, then gradually taking him deeper the more confident she became.

His fingers instinctively tightened in her hair, pulling until she moaned, then guiding her perfect mouth down the length of his shaft, establishing a fast, hot rhythm that she enthusiastically adhered to. Lust seared through his veins, and his stomach muscles tensed as she sucked him to the brink of bliss and the length of his cock pulsed in warning.

She drove him fucking wild, and as much as he loved her efforts, he didn't want to come in her mouth. No, he was determined to be buried as deep inside of her pussy as possible. He wanted to feel her walls clench tight around his cock when she orgasmed right along with him.

He pulled her head back, and when the tip of his dick popped from her mouth, she let out a disappointed little moan. He hauled her back up to her feet and saw the confusion in her eyes, as if she couldn't understand why he didn't let her finish something most guys wouldn't hesitate to take advantage of.

"I need to fuck you," he said, uncaring of

just how aggressive he sounded. "Hard and as deep as I can possibly get."

The answering spark of hunger that lit her eyes was all he needed to see to forge ahead. He was already naked, and he quickly reached behind Jessica and unhooked her bra, yanking the garment down her arms and off. Her enticing breasts spilled free, and he pushed them together, burying his face in her cleavage and taking a few seconds to lick and bite her nipples, until her fingers were gripping his hair and wild, greedy sounds tumbled from her lips.

"One day, I'm going to fuck these gorgeous tits," he growled huskily, reluctantly releasing them and dropping his hands to her hips so he could shove her panties off her body.

Once that was done, he pushed her back onto the bed and moved between her legs, which she'd already spread open for him. She was so wet, her pussy glistening with her arousal, and he was grateful because he couldn't wait a moment longer to fuck her.

He'd had all these sexy plans for tonight, to implement all the *which would you rather* information he'd gleaned from her . . . but after everything he'd been through tonight—with both his parents and Claire—he was beyond desperate to connect with her. Play would come later. This first time, he just needed to claim her, own her, and make sure she knew she was *his*.

He laid his body over hers so that they were face-to-face, her eyes so honest and trusting and filled with desire for him, despite his need to ravish her. Grabbing her wrists, he stretched her arms above her head so that he was completely in control. When he felt his cock nudge into her core, he thrust hard and deep, driving to the hilt inside her.

She cried out—not in pain but pleasure—as she arched her back and anchored her legs around his waist, allowing him to fill her full, again and again. Once he started, he couldn't stop, couldn't slow down, his body demanding he take, take, take . . . and she gave him every-thing he never knew he needed, beyond just physical satisfaction or sublime pleasure.

With her writhing beneath him, her head tipped back and already panting for breath, he knew she was close. As she dug her nails into his skin, her lashes fluttered closed, but he wanted her eyes on him when she came.

"Look at me," he ordered huskily.

She did, and he stared straight into her passion-filled eyes, the raw, vulnerable emotion there slamming into him as hard and deep as the orgasm overwhelming him. The hot clasp of her pussy sent him over the final edge, and he groaned as his entire body stiffened, the force of his release unlike anything he'd experienced before.

After they'd both recovered, he moved off Jessica and she automatically snuggled into his side. He pulled the covers over them, and her soft sigh drifted across his chest while he idly threaded his fingers through her hair, unable to remember when, if ever, he'd felt so content in the aftermath of sex. For the first time ever, Jessica made him feel like he was exactly where he was supposed to be.

He wasn't a guy who believed in insta-love or love at first sight, but he did believe in fate . . . and there was no doubt in his mind that everything in his life had led up to this moment with her. That Jessica was always meant to be his.

Now, he just needed to convince her.

Chapter Seventeen

"What would you like for breakfast?" Jessica asked Derek after they'd shared a shower, dressed for the day—him in his shirt and slacks from the night before and her in a denim skirt and a sweater top—and were heading down to the kitchen together the following morning.

"How about you take me to one of your favorite nearby restaurants so neither one of us has to cook?" he suggested. "One that we can walk to since it's such a nice morning."

She turned and smiled at Derek, feeling like she was glowing from head to toe after her fantastic night with him. "That sounds like a great idea. There's a café close by that I like to go to on the weekends. Millie's. You probably saw it on your morning run last week while you were here."

"Yep, I did," he said with a nod that caused a lock of damp hair to fall across his forehead, making him look adorably boyish. "Let's do it."

They set out, walking along the neighborhood sidewalk toward the small shops and restaurants just outside the residential area, the early-morning sun warming up the October day. Derek took her hand in his, and it all felt so normal, like they were a true couple and this was something they did all the time. Realistically, she knew that this fling between her and Derek wouldn't last forever, not when she knew what he envisioned for his future, and she couldn't guarantee the type of life he pictured for himself. So, for now, she allowed herself to enjoy his company for as long as it lasted, even if it meant her heart and emotions were going to take a hard hit when it all ended.

As they strolled past a house about a block away from hers, Derek lifted his hand and waved at the couple sitting on their porch, each drinking a cup of coffee.

"Hi, George, Maryann," Derek greeted them, surprising Jessica since she didn't even know those neighbors yet.

"Hi, Derek," the older man said jovially. "No run this morning?"

Derek shook his head and grinned. "No, I've got a hungry woman to feed."

"I hope you're heading to Millie's," the woman—Maryann, Jessica assumed—said. "Best breakfast around."

"We are," Derek said cheerfully. "You two have a nice day."

George lifted his coffee mug. "Same to you and your girl."

Jessica gave them a wave, making a mental note to introduce herself to them at another time. Once they were a few houses away, she glanced at Derek curiously. "How do *you* know them?"

"I introduced myself to them last Sunday while I was jogging around the neighborhood," he said with a shrug. "They waved, and so I stopped and chatted with them for a few minutes. Super nice people."

She laughed as they crossed the street on a green light and headed toward the shops and restaurants. "You know my neighbors better than I do."

"I told you I love your neighborhood," he said, reminding her of their conversation last weekend, which had led to a discussion about him wanting to raise kids in an environment like this.

Not wanting to repeat that painful chat about his desire to have a family and kids, she pointed to Millie's, and they walked in that direction. When they arrived, they were early enough that the place wasn't filled yet, and they were seated at an outdoor table in the pleasantly warm sun.

Coffee was a priority, then they ordered their meals—a quiche for her and the lumberjack breakfast for him. The next hour passed with effortless conversation, easy laughter, and flirtatious banter. By the time they returned to her place, Jessica felt as though she'd been given a glimpse of what life and a Sunday morning could be like with Derek.

It was a fantasy she didn't indulge in too deeply.

As they walked into her house, Derek

surprised her by taking her hand and leading her to the couch, where they sat down side by side, his now serious gaze replacing his earlier easygoing demeanor. She wasn't sure what was going on, but the abrupt shift in his mood caused a trickle of unease to course through her.

"Is everything okay?" she asked hesitantly.

He exhaled a deep breath, still holding her hand. "So, before I call an Uber and head home, there's something I've been wanting to talk to you about . . .and it has to do with Claire."

That was the last thing Jessica expected, and just the mention of her nemesis's name made her tense up. "Okay."

He paused for a moment, watching her intently, then spoke. "I noticed at the bachelor auction that there seemed to be something between the two of you, and then again last night, when she said to you 'you might think you got your dream guy, the one you wrote about in your journals' and that tells me that there must be some kind of history between you two, even though you told me that you don't run in the same social circles."

"We don't," she said and tried not to wince at the immediate defensive tone of her voice.

His gaze narrowed. "Then can you explain why there is so much hostility and bitterness between the two of you?"

"Honestly, the hostility and bitterness is all Claire . . . and it goes way back to high school." Jessica stopped from going further, shaking her head and attempting to downplay the dynamic between herself and Claire. "This isn't something I ever wanted to talk about with you. It's awkward because she's your ex, and it's all just so petty."

"She fucking insulted you," he said furiously. "I don't find that just petty but callous and cruel. I saw that side to Claire after I broke things off with her, so I know it exists, but why the fuck is she directing all that hatred toward you after all these years?"

It was obvious to Jessica that Derek was determined to get answers, and knowing there was no way to get around his persistence, she decided to be honest with him. "She hates me because I'm with you and she's not. Because she knew, from that journal of mine that she stole from me back in high school, that I had a crush on you even then, and she doesn't think I deserve to be with a guy like you."

His jaw clenched tight. "What the hell does that mean?"

Jessica leaned back against the couch, gathering her thoughts. "Back in high school, Claire and her girlfriends made me and Avery miserable because we weren't like them. We weren't skinny, we couldn't wear all the latest designer fashions because of our bigger size, and if any of the popular guys even looked our way, it put a bigger target on our backs. She was the quintessential mean girl, and bullying us was her favorite thing to do. She stole my journal, saw the things I wrote about you as my teenage crush, and exploited it all on social media. She was constantly doing crap like that, but the one thing she did that nearly destroyed me was . . ." The painful memory made her stop.

Derek waited for her to continue, and when she didn't, he prompted, "Was what?"

Jessica glanced away, rubbing her palms along her denim-clad thighs, her stomach suddenly in knots, which she hated. But she'd come this far, so she revealed one of her greatest humiliations because she knew she could trust Derek. "Claire persuaded a guy on the football team to pretend he was interested in me. He even asked me to prom, but the night of the dance, when I was dressed in my gown with my makeup and hair all done, and he was supposed to pick me up, he never showed. He deliberately stood me up, and it was all orchestrated by Claire. And for the next month at school, I was the butt of everyone's joke." She swallowed hard and finally met Derek's gaze. "And you want to know what my mother had to say about it?"

He didn't say anything, but she saw the pained look in his eyes, like he knew whatever Jessica would say next would be devastating, and at the age of seventeen, it had been. "My mother told me that if I would just lose weight that I would be beautiful and things like that wouldn't happen to me. As if it was all *my* fault that this dickhead stood me up, when all I wanted from my mother was a hug or some kind of comfort."

Derek scrubbed a hand along his tense jaw, his gaze filled with disbelief. "Jesus Christ," he muttered. "I'm so fucking sorry."

"Those are just some of the highlights, and

I can honestly say that, ten years later, Claire hasn't changed." Jessica absently twisted her fingers in her lap, feeling so vulnerable after giving Derek a glimpse into that part of her past. "Claire clearly wants you back, and she hates that you're dating me, the one girl she always believed she'd never have to compete with."

"It's no competition," he said huskily, his eyes shining with the truth. "You'd win me every single time."

Sitting in the corner of the couch, Derek reached out and grabbed her hand, pulling her into his arms and against his chest. She went willingly, letting his warmth and male scent soothe her. As Derek held her, he gave her the comfort her mother never had, making her feel safe and whole and like she mattered.

It was a feeling she never wanted to end.

Chapter Eighteen

The following Monday afternoon, sitting in the office area in the back of the boutique, Jessica checked the website design for the launch of Curvy Girl Couture Lingerie, which was set to go live in less than two weeks, right when the new line of intimate apparel debuted to the fashion industry. She loved the sensual but modern layout of the site, the sexy new logo, the branding, and especially the tagline across the top that read: *Every woman deserves to feel sexy and desired.*

Jessica grinned, her heart swelling with pride and excitement. That statement, which she'd come up with herself, summed up exactly how she felt about the entire collection of lingerie and her reason for creating each piece. She wanted every woman to know that they were sexy and desirable, no matter their shape or size, and she couldn't wait for her creations to finally become available for purchase. Definitely on this new website and here in the boutique, but also hopefully with Belle Demoiselle, for more exclusive items not available anywhere else.

Exhilaration and indescribable joy filled her, to know that the past year's hard work was so close to becoming a reality. That she'd accomplished something special that would lift a woman's confidence and make her feel beautiful in the process.

Finished with her perusal, she typed her notes and the few minor changes she'd found into an email to the website designer, just as her cellphone started to ping with social media notifications. Wanting to get this information sent before the end of the day, she ignored the annoying alerts.

Jessica finished with the email just as Avery came running into the back room clutching her cell phone, her eyes wide and her expression panicked.

"Oh, my God, Jessica!" Avery exclaimed.

"What is it? What's wrong?" Jessica abruptly stood up from her desk, trying not to panic at her best friend's distraught look. "Avery, is everything okay?"

She shook her head frantically. "No. You need to look at your phone *right now* and any social media notifications that have come through."

"Okay." Worried now, Jessica picked up her phone, unlocked the screen, and was shocked at the number of notifications, all tagging Curvy Girl Couture.

Feeling a trickle of trepidation, she clicked on her Instagram link and sucked in a breath when she saw what was circulating online . . . four *untouched*, not-yet-photoshopped, raw photo images of the women wearing *her* lingerie creations. None of their stretch marks, cellulite or blemishes had been smoothed out, and she immediately recognized the pictures from the recent photo shoot for the Curvy Girl Couture Lingerie catalog and launch. But these weren't the images she had selected for the final campaign, and she couldn't figure out how any of the originals had leaked.

Until she remembered Claire had been in this back room last week, and Jessica had caught her sifting through the pictures. Jessica had startled her and Claire had dropped one of the photos she'd been holding and whirled around, one hand clutching her purse. Clearly, she'd managed to steal a few of the images before Jessica had interrupted her.

With a lump in her throat, Jessica scrolled through the various social media posts, devastated by the ridicule and negative, mean comments directed at the models, who'd been so proud to showcase the lingerie, the loungewear, the seductive boudoir pieces. They didn't deserve to be targeted like this, let alone be humiliated by assholes who believed they were superior in some way. The power of anonymity on the internet, she thought bitterly.

Avery stepped beside her and put an arm around Jessica. There was nothing her best friend could do or say.

In silence, Jessica continued her browsing until she came upon a forward of the original post with the headline, *Not every woman deserves to feel sexy and desired,* an obvious attempt to mock her original slogan.

Jessica couldn't breathe. It was such a personal and direct attack, fueled by online trolls and internet bullies who hid behind random usernames. She felt so helpless as the notification pings continued. The reposting and body shaming snowballed into something so huge there was nothing she could do to stop the onslaught of demeaning, cutting remarks and criticism. Not just of the models but of any woman who didn't fit the ideal mold of current beauty standards.

Her eyes filled with angry tears, and feeling absolutely defeated, she sank back down into her chair because her legs were too wobbly to keep her upright. Avery just stood by her side, her rock until the bitter end, which was coming all too soon. It was only a matter of time before Belle Demoiselle saw the belittling posts that were directly connected to Jessica's lingerie brand . . . and then what?

Everything she'd worked so hard for would come crashing down, and she wasn't sure how she would recover. The emotional toll of the harsh criticism was bad enough, but the damage to her business and her character couldn't be repaired.

Just as Claire no doubt intended.

* * *

Sitting at his desk at work, Derek sent off an email and opened another to respond to an inter-office question from the contracts department. His cellphone rang and he glanced at his sister's name flashing on the screen. He immediately picked up. She was one of the few people in his life he'd put everything aside for, including business.

"Hey, Nikki, what's up?" he asked, reclining in his chair.

"I know you have zero connections or interest in the online fashion industry, but you need to know that Jessica and her upcoming lingerie line are being trolled on social media."

He frowned, trying to understand his sister's words, which confused the hell out of him. "What are you talking about?"

She took a deep breath to calm down before speaking again. "Someone got ahold of unedited photos of the models wearing Jessica's lingerie designs and leaked them to social media and fashion influencers. They're *untouched* pictures," she stressed. "I don't know how to explain it any better, but every stretch mark, fat bulge, and dimple is out there for the world to see. Which means catty bitches are having a fucking field day raking Jessica and these models over the coals. It's like bullying to the nth degree."

His sister rarely cursed. Their mother had seen to that, but she did now to express the importance of what had happened. Derek straightened in his chair and attempted to make sense of the situation. "How do you know this?"

"Because I'm a former model and most of my social media is fashion stuff and it's splashed all over my accounts!" Her voice rose with her impatience. "And the demeaning, offensive comments are awful and I can't imagine how devastated Jessica must be over this smear campaign. I wanted you to know because it's bad, Derek. *Really* bad."

The urgency in his sister's voice left no doubt in Derek's mind that she wasn't exaggerating. He swore under his breath and immediately knew what he had to do. Get to Jessica as soon as possible and find out if she was okay.

"Thanks, Nik. I'll call you later." He ended the call and tried reaching Jessica, but she didn't pick up her phone, so he immediately started for his office door, pulling up the Uber app. A car would be the quickest way to reach her.

"Hey, where are you off to in a hurry?" Ben asked as Derek passed him in the hallway.

"To see your sister," he said, not bothering to stop and waste time explaining things. Jessica was his priority.

Ben followed him into the receptionist area. "Wait, you can't leave. We have a marketing meeting in twenty minutes."

"I don't give a shit," Derek said over his shoulder. "There's an issue on social media involving Jessica and someone sabotaging Curvy Girl Couture, and she needs me." *Even if she didn't know it or wouldn't admit it.* It was important for him to be there for her through this crisis because, sure as shit, her mother wouldn't offer any kind of support.

"Oh, hell," Ben said, concern deepening his tone. "You're right. I'll handle the meeting. Keep me posted and let me know if you need me for anything."

By the time Derek rode the elevator down to the ground floor of the building and walked out of the lobby, his car was waiting for him at the curb. He slid into the back, and while the guy navigated traffic to Jessica's store, Derek clicked on the few links that Nikki had forwarded to him so he could see for himself how online trolls took such delight in tearing other people down.

Nikki was right and Derek's stomach twisted into knots at the sight. This was huge and possibly damaging to Jessica's upcoming lingerie launch and campaign. It was the kind of coverage that would cause a major brand to pull out and walk away.

When he arrived at the boutique, he stormed inside, grateful that the only person he encountered in the showroom was Maddie, who looked completely stricken, her eyes filled with unshed tears.

She pointed to the back area of the store, obviously realizing why he was there. "She's in the back."

He didn't stop his stride until he reached Jessica, who glanced at him with red-rimmed, pain-filled eyes. Her eyeliner was smeared and his heart ached, seeing her utterly destroyed.

Ignoring Avery, Derek pulled Jessica into his arms. She didn't resist his embrace, for which he was grateful. Instead, she sagged against him, seemingly absorbing his comfort and strength, which he was more than willing to give.

He held her for a long while, nodding at Avery when she motioned to the front of the store and left them alone. He rubbed her back until he felt the tension ease from her body.

After a few more moments, he let her go and stepped back, needing to know the details so he could figure out how to handle the problem for her. The desire to protect her was overwhelming, and he'd do whatever it took to find out who was responsible and defuse the toxic mess. He had the money, the resources, and the connections to make the perpetrator's life fucking miserable.

"What the hell is going on?" he asked, his voice low and gruff. He didn't bother asking if she was okay. Clearly, she wasn't fine after being annihilated on social media.

She blinked up at him in surprise. "How did you know to come by?"

"Nikki called and told me. As soon as I found out, I came right over. How did this happen?" And the bigger question, why would someone do this to her?

She crossed her arms over her chest and her cheeks turned red, her despair turning to fury. "My best guess? Claire leaked the unfinished photos."

He opened his mouth, then snapped it shut again. *Jesus Christ.* Of course this linked back to Claire. "How?"

Jessica exhaled a deep breath. "She came by here last week, after my weekend with you. Her friends were at the nightclub, and they sent her photos of us together. We were dancing and close, and Claire informed me I should end things with you before things ended badly for *me*. I didn't take her seriously but I guess this is what she meant."

Fury lanced through him. "Why didn't you tell me she was here?"

He growled the question out of pure frustration, causing Jessica to stubbornly raise her chin. "Because I handled it and her," she replied.

He jammed his fingers through his hair, wishing she would have confided in him rather than kept that unpleasant visit to herself. But his strong-willed, beautiful Jessica didn't want to rely on him, and it was both admirable and exasperating.

"And how did she get the photos?" he asked, trying to piece it all together.

"They were out on the drafting table when she was here," Jessica said, indicating the work area. "Not knowing our history, Maddie let her wait for me back here, and when I walked in, Claire was going through the photos. At the time, I didn't know she'd slipped a few of them into her purse, but Avery and I just pulled up the security feed for this back room on the day that Claire was here. You can clearly see she took them before I arrived."

She showed him her laptop, a grainy but unmistakable image of Claire in this back room pulled up on the screen. She clicked a button, and the video played, showing Claire taking the photos and putting them in her purse one by one, obviously not realizing her actions were being recorded.

"Un-fucking-believable," he muttered through clenched teeth.

Jessica picked up her cell and opened an app. "And about half an hour ago, Avery saw this picture on Claire's Instagram page. That's one of her friends who's a fashion influencer."

She turned the screen toward him, revealing a snapshot of Claire taking a selfie of them at a bar in downtown Manhattan, smirking and holding up drinks in a toast with the caption "Success!" The post had been uploaded within the past hour, including the name and location of the establishment since Claire was one of those women who wanted everyone to know she was at the swankiest place in the city.

Rage bubbled up inside him that Claire would go to such lengths to tear Jessica down so completely, then fucking *brag* about it and celebrate another woman's ruin.

"Fuck," he growled, feeling feral. "I'm going to make sure she regrets leaking those photos."

He turned to go do just that since he knew

where she was, but Jessica grabbed his arm, stopping him.

"Derek, don't," she said, her tone firm, despite everything she'd just been through. "This is not your battle to fight."

"*You're* my battle to fight!" He'd burn down the fucking city for her if that's what it took to take away this pain and hurt Claire had inflicted.

"No, I'm not." Her eyes were soft with gratitude, but there was no mistaking the determination in her tone. "As much as I appreciate you wanting to defend me, I need to handle this my own way. But not now. Not tonight. I'm too upset and I don't want to say or do anything that will make this entire situation worse."

She was being smart and reasonable, while he wanted to strangle his ex for hurting Jessica. "You're coming home with me."

She straightened her shoulders, that damned pride back again. "I don't need—"

"Yes, you *do* need me," he argued, trying to find a balance to allow her to maintain her dignity yet know she wasn't alone. Not ever again. "I won't fight your battles, but I will be there for you. You're just too fucking stubborn to admit you want me here."

Her eyes widened in shock, and he softened his words by brushing his knuckles gently down the soft curve of her cheek. "I'm not letting you go home alone to torture yourself all night long over something you can't change." He sighed and put his forehead to hers, taking the frustration out of his voice. "I'm not giving you a choice, because I need you, too. I need to know that you're okay. So, gather whatever you need, and let's go."

He watched her struggle with some kind of internal conflict, one part of her trying to be strong and another wanting to give in to his care. She was wary of depending on another person. Even him.

"It's fine, Jessica," Avery said, having come into the back room at some point and overhearing their conversation. "He's right. There's nothing you can do from here that will change things. Not tonight, anyway. Take a change of clothes off the rack for tomorrow, and go with Derek. Stay off of social media and try to decompress. Maddie and I will close up."

"Okay," she finally said, the stiffness in her shoulders easing as she gave in.

Relief surged through him as she gathered her laptop and a few other items into a carrying case, then selected an outfit to wear the next day since she wouldn't be going home.

She was quiet on the ride to his place, staring out the passenger window. Instead of forcing conversation, he allowed her the time she needed to think. There was no point in making small talk or even rehashing what had happened, which would only increase her anxiety. All Derek cared about was that she was with him and that she knew she wasn't alone.

They arrived at his building, and she followed him past the doorman to the elevator, which they rode up to the top floor. The steel doors opened into his penthouse suite, and he set her things on the couch while she glanced around.

He'd only recently purchased the apartment, so it was sparsely decorated. Just the basics and necessities so far, and she silently walked to the floor-to-ceiling windows overlooking the New York City skyline. While she stared at the view, still lost in thought, he placed an order for dinner from a nearby Chinese restaurant, selecting a few of their popular dishes so there would be plenty to choose from.

A short while later, their meal was delivered, and while he ate a good amount, Jessica merely picked at her food, clearly not having much of an appetite. Her silence continued, and after a while, it grated but there was nothing he could say. Afterward, he cleaned up, settled them on the couch, and turned on a random TV show, knowing whatever he selected wouldn't matter much to Jessica. She stared blankly at the screen, still utterly despondent, and his heart hurt just watching her.

There was no cheering her up, no distracting her from the troubling thoughts tumbling through her mind. Nothing he could say or do to reassure her that everything would be okay, because that wasn't a promise he could keep. And it made him feel fucking helpless, because he knew how scared she was to lose everything she'd worked so hard to achieve. All because of one person's vindictive streak caused by Jessica getting involved with him.

Jessica adhered to Avery's request to stay off social media for the evening. She didn't obsessively check her phone or scroll through the notifications still randomly pinging, which had slowed considerably as the night went on. Thank God.

After watching a few shows, she finally relaxed against him, and he decided it was time to call it a night. "Let's go to bed."

She didn't argue, just followed him into the main bedroom.

He gave her a new toothbrush and one of his T-shirts to wear, and she disappeared into the bathroom, returning a short while later, looking way too tempting in his shirt. She'd washed off her makeup, leaving her skin smooth and pink. She still looked incredibly beautiful.

He was already in bed, wearing a pair of pajama bottoms, and he pulled back the covers and patted the mattress beside him. She slid in and he turned off the lights, then he secured an arm around her waist and spooned her from behind, his head resting on the pillow beside hers.

All he intended was to comfort her, but his

body was still completely aware of hers—the way her ass felt pressed against his dick, how close his hand was to her breast, and the feminine scent permeating her skin. He swallowed back a groan and attempted to force his mind to non-arousing thoughts.

"Thank you." She finally spoke, her voice quiet in the dark.

"For?" he asked.

"Taking care of me." She slid her hand along his arm, down to the hand resting on her stomach, and intimately entwined their fingers. "And for not letting me be alone tonight," she admitted.

"You don't *ever* have to be alone," he said. And he meant it.

If he had his way, when all this shit was over, he'd make sure she knew just how serious he was about that statement.

Chapter Nineteen

Jessica woke up cocooned in the warmth of Derek's arms. Contentment and a sense of security rolled through her . . . until she remembered that her life was in shambles. Her character had been defamed, her business maligned, and her new lingerie line was probably in jeopardy—not just the upcoming launch but Belle Demoiselle's interest in acquiring an exclusive line of designs. Once they saw all the negative press, she doubted they'd want any association with her or her creations.

"You're awake," Derek murmured from behind her.

"How did you know?" She hadn't made a sound or moved.

"Your body went from relaxed and peaceful to tense, so I'm assuming you're back in your head again." The hand around her waist slid to her hip, and he caressed her curves, attempting to soothe her.

She rolled to her back, not wanting to get distracted by Derek's slow, sensual touch. As much as she desired him, enjoying sex right now was impossible. "Time to face the music and figure out what the hell I'm going to do."

Still lying on his side, he propped his head on his hand, a small smile lifting his lips. "As much as I want to jet you off to somewhere private to forget about all this shit, I know you're right. Just know that, as terrible as things may seem right now, this will blow over."

"But at what cost?" she asked, hearing the fear in her voice.

He gave her an understanding look, but he had no reassuring answers, nor did she expect any. A pat reply like *It's going to be okay* wasn't true at the moment, and he was smart enough to know that she wouldn't want to be patronized.

Dreading what awaited her, she reached for her phone, which she'd left on the nightstand before going to bed. She'd turned the ringer on silent for the night so the pinging sounds wouldn't keep her awake, and as she unlocked the screen and saw the sheer volume of new notifications, her stomach sank. She'd hoped that the frenzy would subside overnight. Clearly, that wasn't the case.

Even as she watched, new notifications kept popping up on her screen. Avery had tried to call her numerous times that morning, and her friend had also left a voice message. Bracing herself for more bad news, Jessica hit play on the recording and put the phone to her ear.

"Oh, my God, pick up your phone already!" Avery nearly shrieked, making Jessica wince at the urgency in her tone. "And when you get this message, look at your notifications and the response to the photos that were leaked on social media yesterday!"

Jessica glanced at Derek, hesitating, because the last thing she wanted was for him to witness her having another meltdown while she read through the mean posts and comments.

Avery had screamed her message and Derek had been able to hear. Understanding glimmered in his eyes as he leaned over and softly kissed her lips. "Take your time. I'll be out in the kitchen making us some coffee if you need me." He rolled to his side of the bed and got up, giving her time and space to deal with whatever was on social media this morning.

He walked out and her gaze lingered on his strong, muscled backside until he disappeared from view. Then, gathering her resolve, she sat against the headboard and clicked on the first notification, confused when it took her to a well-known celebrity's page.

There was a picture of the actress—who'd been called out for being "chunky" in a previous role—wearing nothing more than a bra and panties, a fierce and proud look on her face. She'd tagged Curvy Girl Couture, and the caption beneath the photo read, *This is what realistic beauty looks like.*

Jessica's heart pounded in her chest as she opened another notification and tag and saw a snapshot of a famous plus-size model in a swim-suit, baring her beautiful curves, right along with her cellulite and stretch marks. *Sexy comes in all shapes and sizes. Be proud of who and what you are!*

Every notification this morning led to a post with body-positivity comments and photos. Dozens of celebrities, influencers, and even female athletes had joined the movement, canceling out the disparaging, offensive remarks from yesterday with their uplifting, positive affirmations. Even men had joined in, posting photos of their girlfriends or wives in their favorite lingerie, announcing, *Real men love curves!*

The comments beneath the original post of the untouched Curvy Girl Couture Lingerie photos were now overrun with inspiring messages: *Love how beautiful and natural these women are! Love your body unconditionally!* And so many more comments just as positive, Jessica couldn't read them all.

She scrolled some more and saw a post on Belle Demoiselle's social media page responding to yesterday's frenzy. *Curvy Girl Couture keeps it real!*

Even Jessica's DMs were overflowing with supportive messages.

She shrieked, just as Avery had. She

laughed and cried at the same time, elation and gratitude filling her, and she needed to share the news.

She jumped out of bed and ran to the kitchen, catching Derek walking toward the bedroom. "Derek, look!"

"What's wrong? Why did you scream?" Worry lines creased his forehead, his expression turning curious as he studied her face. "You're laughing . . . and you're crying. I'm not sure what to make of that."

She laughed again. "It's all good, I swear," she said, then turned her phone screen toward him, showing him one of the celebrity posts. "*Look.*"

He glanced at the picture, then read the caption, his eyes going wide. "Holy shit. That's amazing."

She showed him half a dozen more, enough for him to realize that Claire's smear campaign and her attempt to sabotage Jessica's business and upcoming lingerie line had backfired. In a big way.

"So, I take it you'll be eating breakfast this morning?" he asked with a grin.

"Yes," she said, her mood boosted with a rush of adrenaline. "I'm starved!"

She made herself a cup of coffee and sat down at the small dining table, scrolling through all the supportive posts and comments that spread nothing but kindness, altruism, and social consciousness within each community. Her spirits were totally uplifted, and while Derek made breakfast, she attempted to respond to many of the DMs streaming in, feeling overwhelmed but also grateful for the viral celebrity endorsements that now dominated social media.

A short while later, Derek set a plate in front of her, and Jessica was surprised to see French toast along with a small bowl of fresh berries and cream. She set her phone down and smiled at him as he sat across the table from her, his own dish piled high.

"You said you couldn't cook," she said, slathering butter on the thick, fragrant piece of pan-fried bread. "I think you were holding out on me."

"When it comes to dinners, not so much," he said with a shrug, drawing her gaze to his still-bare chest. "Breakfast is pretty straight-forward."

She took a bite, the cinnamon, nutmeg, and maple syrup all mingling on her tongue. "It's delicious."

A few more bites in, Jessica set her fork down on her plate and met his gaze. "You do realize that I need to confront Claire about what she did."

Jessica wasn't asking for permission, just giving him a heads-up regarding what she intended to do. Claire had hurt too many people with her spite—including the models in the pictures she'd stolen—and Jessica wasn't about to let the other woman get away with her behavior. Even if it had ultimately worked in Jessica's favor.

Derek opened his mouth, she assumed to argue or take charge and insist on confronting Claire himself, but then closed it again and sat back in his seat. "Are you going to set up a meeting with her?" he asked, and she knew what it cost him to let her handle the situation herself.

"No. I don't want to give her time to prepare. Claire caught me off guard, so there's

JUST A LITTLE HOOKUP

no reason why I can't do the same to her. She
always posts her whereabouts on social media,
so I'll just wait for the right time and place."

The right time and place came much
sooner than Jessica anticipated. An hour and a
half later, after Jessica had showered and was
getting ready to head to the boutique, Claire's
Instagram showed her most recent post. An
"outfit of the day" photo, along with the
caption: *Heading out for lunch at Sadelle's.*

Of course she'd mentioned the trendy
hotspot, which wasn't too far from Derek's
apartment. In the picture she'd posted, Claire
looked very subdued—unlike yesterday's
giddy celebratory photo with her influencer
friend—but not defeated, considering the twist
in fate she'd no doubt woken up to. No,
someone like Claire wouldn't show a crack in
her armor and would act as though her
scheme hadn't turned around and bitten her
in the ass. Which meant dressing up in her
designer finest and fake smiling for her
phone's camera so her followers believed her
life was a charmed one.

Jessica couldn't wait to wipe that smug look
off the other woman's face.

"Are you sure you want to do this?" Derek asked, looking down at her screen.

She glanced up. He was dressed in a dark brown suit for work, which made his green eyes even sexier. It was after eleven a.m., and he'd already let Ben know that he'd be late to the office.

She didn't miss the concern in his voice or the protective way he placed his palms on her hips. "I have to." She smoothed her hand down the lapel of his suit jacket, the heady scent of his cologne warring with her desire to drag him back to the bedroom and have her way with him. "Or else you and I both know that this bullying will never end."

"*I* could end it," he growled fiercely.

"Thank you, but no," she said, patting his chest. "I love that you want to be my knight in shining armor, but I refuse to be cowed by a bully, and she needs to know not to mess with me."

"That's my girl," he said, his voice now low and intimate. "As much as I want to beat my chest like a caveman, I respect that you need to do this your way."

She laughed and came up on her toes to

place a kiss on his cheek. "It's important to me, and I appreciate you keeping your baser instincts under control," she teased.

His lashes fell as he gave her a seductive look. "Fine. I'll save the dominating for the bedroom."

They headed down to the lobby together, then went their separate ways. His car went to his office, and hers followed the route to Sadelle's. Jessica had no idea who she'd find with Claire—most likely one or two of her friends—which didn't matter to Jessica. The whole online world already had a front seat to her humiliation at Claire's hands, so what were a few of her friends to witness Claire's disgrace?

Jessica walked into Sadelle's, wearing the black pencil skirt she'd taken from the boutique last night and a burgundy blouse. Knowing that reservations were required at the restaurant, she smiled at the hostess and mentioned that she was meeting Claire Sutherland. The young woman pointed in the direction that she would find her table.

With her chin high and her shoulders pulled back, Jessica walked through the establishment, surprised by who she saw sitting with Claire. Derek's mother, Collette, and Claire's mother, Olivia, were at the table. The women were close friends and had hoped to marry off Derek and Claire. A sudden twisting of nerves hit Jessica's stomach, but she refused to let the unexpected guests deter her from her mission.

They seemed to be at the end of their meal, and while the two older women chatted away, Claire sat with a sullen look on her face, pushing her food around on her plate and looking like she'd rather be anywhere but there. Without announcing herself, Jessica slid into the one empty chair at the table, right across from Claire.

Both women stopped talking and stared at her with confused frowns, while Claire's expression immediately turned wary.

"Hello, ladies," Jessica said in a polite, friendly manner. "Do you mind if I join you for a few minutes? I need to talk to Claire and this shouldn't take very long."

Derek's mother's lips pursed in disapproval. "We were just finishing up lunch," she said, her tone dismissive.

"Even better, so I don't ruin anyone's

appetite since you've already eaten," Jessica said with a smile, keeping her entire demeanor cordial.

She might be there to confront Claire, but she wasn't going to give these women any ammunition to use against her later by raising her voice or making a scene. As far as anyone around them could see or hear, they were just having a polite conversation.

"Aren't you the woman who came with Derek to the fundraiser last weekend?" Olivia asked, disdain in her tone.

"Yes, I am," she replied, folding her hands in front of her as she glanced across the table and met Claire's narrowed gaze. "It was a lovely evening."

Claire seemed to draw herself up, straightening her shoulders, and Jessica recognized the cruel glint that flickered her eyes. "I'm so sorry to hear about what happened online with those untouched photos being leaked," she said, her tone sugary sweet.

Bitch. Did she really think she could cover up what she'd done with her innocent act? "No, you're not sorry," Jessica countered.

Collette gasped. "Well, that was rude."

"It's the truth," Jessica said, not taking her eyes off of Claire. "Would you like to tell them what you did, or should I?"

Panic flashed across Claire's face. "I have no idea what you're talking about."

"Then let me refresh your memory with something more visual." Jessica reached into her purse for the photos she'd printed out showing shots of Claire in Jessica's office, taking the photos and putting them in her bag. Jessica pushed them across the table for everyone to see. "That's you, stealing the same pictures that were leaked to social media."

All three women stared in horror at the irrefutable evidence Jessica had just presented, their expressions almost comical except no one was laughing. Because there was no denying the proof in front of them.

Keeping her smile sweet and her voice calm, Jessica said, "If you disparage me or my business ever again, I will take these photos to the police. Corporate espionage is a crime, and I won't hesitate to expose you if you make that mistake again."

Claire's eyes were huge and swirling with anger. "Are you *threatening* me?" she hissed, and though her voice was low, there was no doubt she was about to spiral.

Her mother put a hand on Claire's arm to keep her calm, no doubt because she did not want to draw attention to her daughter creating a scene.

"Of course not," Jessica said in a placating tone, the kind that indicated Claire was being ridiculous with her accusation. "I'm just giving you a friendly reminder not to mess with me and what's mine, or next time there will be consequences."

"Derek isn't *yours*," Claire sneered, the bitter words spewing out, despite the fact that both mothers watched in panicked silence.

Jessica recognized Claire's last-ditch effort to cut her down, and she found it sad. "I refuse to fight with you over a man. I'm not going to stoop that low, and besides, I don't have to. Derek makes his own choices, and he's already told me that he'd pick me every time," she said, unable to forget their earlier conversation.

The other woman had no response to that, and she sat in silence, fury evident in her narrowed eyes and pinched expression. But

Jessica had the upper hand, and there was nothing more Claire could do.

Having said her piece, Jessica stood, and she was unable to hold back one last comment. "I suppose I should thank you for leaking those photos and for all the free press for Curvy Girl Couture. I never thought I'd have *actual celebrities* endorsing my designs and supporting my business. So, thank you for that invaluable word of mouth."

While Claire continued to fume in frustrated, angry silence, Jessica nodded courteously at Olivia, then turned to Derek's mother. "Mrs. Bettencourt, it was nice to see you again," she said. "Enjoy the rest of your afternoon, ladies."

Jessica walked out of the restaurant, her legs a bit shaky but her entire being filled with so much satisfaction. She'd stood up for herself, defended her self-worth, and now she refused to allow any more toxicity into her life, not when she had so many amazing things to look forward to.

She hailed a cab, slipped into the backseat, and gave the driver directions to the Blackout Media offices, where Derek was waiting to hear how her confrontation with Claire had gone. She planned to assure him she'd handled his ex and tell him how she'd faced Claire and stood up for herself.

Then she needed to be that brave with him. She needed to have the courage to be vulnerable and take the emotional risks she'd avoided for most of her life. The kind that could leave her with either a broken heart or the greatest love of her life.

And that meant being honest with herself and with Derek. She was in love with him. Had been for most of her life, and she wanted more than random hookups with him. She wanted a commitment and a future, not a temporary fling, and she wasn't going to settle for anything less. But the choice wasn't solely hers. Derek, too, deserved the future he envisioned for himself. Even if that meant she couldn't be a part of it, and her throat grew tight at the painful thought.

Derek had proven he was a good friend and her white knight—and she knew he always would be, no matter what happened between them. He was that honorable, that dependable and loyal. And those were just a few of the qualities she loved about him. But Derek wanted something she might not ever be able to give him, and she had to be prepared because her heart and love might not be enough to make up for the possibility that she couldn't provide him with the family he desired.

The driver arrived at the building, and Jessica got out of the cab, shoring up the last of her courage to find out what kind of future awaited her . . . one with ... or without Derek.

Chapter Twenty

Feeling anxious and impatient, Derek paced in front of the windows in his office while checking his cellphone every few minutes for some kind of message from Jessica. He had the sound on as loud as possible for any calls or pings, but that didn't stop him from obsessively looking to see if something, anything, had come through.

They'd parted ways over an hour ago, and while he was proud as hell of her for confronting Claire on her own, he couldn't help but worry about how the meeting would go. Or how it might end. Even while he had every bit of confidence that Jessica could handle the situation and Claire, he hated not being by there to defend the woman he loved.

Love . . . the word and undeniable emotion resonated inside him, settling in his chest along with the certainty that Jessica was always meant to be his. And if he had his way, now that she was *in* his life, he wouldn't ever let her go.

His phone rang, and without even looking at the caller, he swiped the bar and put the unit up to his ear. "Hello?"

"How could you allow Jessica to make a scene with Claire at Sadelle's?" His mother's irritated voice came through loud and clear. "I was there with Olivia when she sat down at our table and started making all sorts of horrible accusations. Did you know about this?"

Un-fucking-believable. Of course his mother had been there and refused to believe the black-and-white proof. "Did I know about what, Mom?" he snapped. "That Claire sabotaged Jessica's campaign by leaking unauthorized photos online that she stole? Or maybe that Claire had bullied Jessica since high school? Or wait, did I know about Claire threatening Jessica to stop dating me or things would end badly for her? Are any of those things enough for you to choose from, or do you need a few more?"

"Don't be so sarcastic," his mother said in that pretentious tone he hated.

He ignored her comment. "It's not an accusation, it's the *truth* and I'm sure Jessica showed you the proof."

His mother was quiet for a moment, then came back with, "If she's trying to ruin Claire's reputation—"

He barked out an incredulous laugh. "Claire has already done that to herself."

"I don't know why you're sticking up for Jessica—"

Oh, he'd had enough. "I'm sticking up for her because she was *wronged* by what Claire did," he shouted back, certain his hard, stomping pacing would leave grooves in his office carpet.

"Well, maybe you ought to listen to Claire's side of things," his mother said. "That maybe the only reason she did it was because she loves you and you wouldn't listen or give her another chance."

"So it's my fault she can't take no for an

answer? That she resorted to stealing and attempting to destroy another woman's reputation for her own gain?" He jammed his fingers through his hair, feeling as though he wanted to rip out a few strands in frustration and anger. "She doesn't love *me*. She loves my money and the social status it gives her, and the fact that she'd tear someone down to get what she wants —*someone I care about*—is unforgiveable."

His mother made a sound of disgust. "I really don't know what you see in *that girl*."

Derek wasn't going to justify her comment with a response. "I'm done with this conversation, and I'm done with you interfering in my life. Just like Nikki, I'm *done*. I am dating Jessica, so get fucking used to it." He disconnected the call and resisted the urge to throw his phone across the room.

Out of the corner of his eye, he caught movement at the open doorway and thought it was his secretary until he turned and saw Jessica standing there. Her big, round eyes told him that she'd caught a good portion of that heated conversation.

"God, she's horrendous," he said, already

calmer now that Jessica was here and he could see for himself she was okay. He strode across the room and pulled her into his arms for a hug, which she tentatively returned.

When he pulled back and really looked at her face, he noticed her gaze and expression were guarded. He was so used to Jessica being mostly an open book, and his chest tightened with unease. "Are you okay?" he asked.

"Yes, I'm good," she replied, and while she was outwardly fine, it was the emotional issues that concerned him. She was more subdued than he'd ever seen her.

Thinking maybe she needed a bit of space after what she'd just gone through, he walked back to his desk and set his phone on the surface, but he couldn't avoid what she'd overheard.

"So ..." He turned around and rested his backside against the edge of the desk. "My mother just gave me her skewed version of events," he said in a wry tone. "But I want you to tell me the truth about what happened at Sadelle's."

Keeping her distance, which he didn't like

at all, she explained everything from the moment she walked into the restaurant to her triumphant exit. Clearly, she'd slayed and owned the confrontation, and he was so damn proud of her for keeping her cool while definitely making her point.

When she was done, she walked to his office door and closed it behind her. Though he wished she had something sexy in mind to celebrate her victory, when she turned to him, her serious expression made his gut clench with panic.

She lifted her solemn gaze to his as she approached. "I was, uh, hoping you and I could talk."

His throat suddenly felt dry, and he swallowed hard, trying not to assume the worst, which was difficult with the reserved vibes she was giving off. He was so used to Jessica's vibrant personality and her vivacious spirit, and this cool side of her made him feel like she was trying to put as much emotional distance between them as possible.

"Talk about what?" he asked, resisting the urge to grab her and haul her into his arms.

"This thing between us," she said, twisting her hands in front of her, revealing the doubts and insecurities she was fighting.

Oh, yeah, he knew exactly where this conversation was headed, and he refused to let her end their relationship. As much as he wanted to take charge and explain his vision of their future, he needed to hear her out. "This *thing*?" he asked, refusing to let her minimize their feelings without calling her out.

She visibly swallowed. "A fling. A hookup. An affair. Whatever you want to call it."

Oh, fuck.

This he hadn't seen coming. The fact that she was reducing what they'd shared down to something insignificant.

He hadn't asked her for a commitment because he'd thought pressure would scare her off. She had serious insecurities when it came to men and a deep-rooted fear of not being good enough. He'd thought he'd take time to build and solidify their relationship. To show her what she meant to him, how serious he was about her, before taking that next step. And he'd wanted to talk to her brother and promise him he would put Jessica's happiness first. Always. Since Ben hadn't decked him after that first conversation, Derek had waited because Jessica had her new lingerie launch coming up and he'd wanted her to be able to focus.

Then, he'd planned to reveal his feelings.

Now, he realized the error of that decision. His fingers gripped the edge of the desk. "What about our ... *fling?*" he forced himself to ask, knowing he had to listen without jumping to conclusions.

She lifted her chin as she faced him. "I want more. I *deserve* more. From you."

"Yes, you do." He let out a relieved breath, wanting nothing more than to spank her for scaring him so damned badly. "I want more, too."

Her eyes flashed with relief of her own. "I love you," she blurted out in a rush. "I thought it was years of infatuation because of my teenage crush on you, but being with you now . . . I know it's always been love. And I know you care about me, too."

He did. Oh, God, *he did*, and he'd never deny the truth. He straightened, prepared to put his own feelings out in the open. "Jessica, I—"

She put up a hand to stop him, shaking her head, her eyes still showing her turbulent emotions and vulnerabilities he hadn't yet been able to conquer.

"Let me finish," she said, her voice raspy. "I do love you . . . but sometimes love isn't enough, and I know you want a different future than what I might be able to give you."

He frowned in confusion. "What are you talking about?"

She exhaled a deep breath, her expression pained. "Family . . . kids . . ."

"And?" He was missing something huge and he didn't understand.

She shot him an exasperated look. "I told you, but it probably didn't compute because we weren't serious at the time, but my PCOS? I can't promise that you'd ever have a biological child with me."

He blinked at her in shock, surprised she'd even think this would be an issue for him. "Jessica, I want *you*. I'm not asking you to have kids."

"Right now, no, you aren't," she agreed.

"But in the future, it could be a deal breaker for you, and I'd rather know now than have my heart broken worse later on."

He exhaled a long breath, finally understanding all her years of insecurities and fears. Yet despite them, she was putting her heart in his hands and he knew what he had to do.

Needing to touch her, he closed the distance between them and reached for her wringing fingers, separating them and holding her hands in his. "Jessica, look at me."

She lifted her head, hope and doubt clashing in her eyes.

"Here's a few things you need to know," he said, his tone gruff and serious. "One, I'm in this for the long haul. I'm as serious as it gets about you. Like, I'm *all* in." He tightened his hold on her hands. "And second, *you* are enough for me, sweetheart. I don't give a damn about anything else. Just you, and me, together, wherever we decide this ends up. And third and most importantly, if we decide we want kids and you can't get pregnant, there are other ways to create a family. As long as we decide together, we will be fine. A biological child is not deal breaker for me."

She bit her bottom lip, her beautiful eyes filling with tears. She opened her mouth to speak, but he wasn't done.

"You and I haven't been dating long, but you *know* me and who I am," he insisted. "What you see is what you get . . . and I hope what you see is a man who is crazy about you. Who adores every perfect part of you. Your smile, your creativity, your determination, and your ability to face adversity. But you don't have to face *any* hardships alone, because I'm right here for you, and I'm not going anywhere."

A tear slipped free, and he gently wiped it away with the pad of his thumb, touching her as if she were the most precious thing in his life, because she was.

"I love you," he said, needing her to hear the words, which seemed to cause another rush of moisture to fill her eyes. "Those better be tears of happiness," he said, causing her to nod and laugh. "Good. And just so you know, I'm so fucking glad you bought me at the bachelor auction, because I'd probably spend the rest of my life trying to find a woman exactly like you.

And there is only one *you*, Jessica, and you're mine."

A joyful smile burst across her lips, and she flung herself at him, her arms wrapping around his neck as she hugged him tight. Relief flooded him and he secured an arm around her waist. He ran his free hand over the nape of her neck, gently massaging there.

"We'll figure it out," he promised in her ear. "Every step of the way. Together."

"Okay," she said and released him, but he wasn't ready to put any space between.

He framed her face in his hands and brought her mouth to his, kissing her like she was the air he breathed—slow and deep and thoroughly. Desire filled him, along with the need to spread her out on his desk and show her that she belonged to him.

His hands wandered along the curve of her hip and around to her ass . . . until the door to his office opened and someone cleared their throat.

Startled by the interruption, Jessica jumped back, turning around to see her brother standing in the doorway, his brows raised high.

A look of wide-eyed panic flashed across her now flushed face at being caught.

"Uh, I just thought I'd come in and see if Jessica was okay," Ben said, a smirk lifting his lips. "I saw her walk into the office earlier, but I was on the phone. Clearly, she's in good hands, so, as you were," he said, waving playfully, and stepped back out of the room, closing the door behind him.

Jessica glanced back at Derek, shaking her head. "Why didn't my brother lose his shit after catching you kissing me?"

Derek grinned. "Because I already told him I wanted to see where things went with us. Right after our weekend together. I wasn't going to date you behind his back."

She blinked at him. "And he's okay with it?"

"Clearly, he is." Derek chuckled and pulled her right back into his arms, and this time she went willingly, melting against him perfectly. "Not that it would matter. I'm willing to risk everything for you, Jessica."

"You are full of surprises." She released a soft, dreamy little sigh and smiled at him.

"Mmm," he said, more interested in going

back to pre-interrupted activities. "Now, where were we?"

She put his hands back on her ass, then touched her lips to his. "Right here."

He pulled her against him and groaned, so glad they were in agreement. This *thing* between them was so much more than just a little hookup, and he planned to spend the rest of their lives together proving it.

Epilogue

"Oh, my God, oh, my God," Avery said, sounding as though she was about to hyperventilate. "That's *Ashley Graham* over there! She's freaking *here* at your lingerie debut, talking to the press about *your* new line of designs for Curvy Girl Couture Lingerie!"

Jessica laughed, feeling giddy, which had nothing to do with the one glass of champagne she'd had. "I know, I'm shocked, too." She was still trying to process the overwhelming success of her lingerie line, which had exploded with interest after the internet debacle.

When Rachel Cohen, a popular plus-size fashion influencer, asked if she could bring a guest with her to the launch, Jessica had no idea it would be such a huge name in the full-figure modeling world. But here Ashley Graham was, gracious and sweet and also exuberant about spreading body positivity and supporting Jessica's new venture.

Everything about the evening was surreal, and Jessica was floating on air. The after-party, which had been followed by a fashion show with all her models—including the ones who'd been a part of the online debacle that had turned into a success—was packed with huge names in the industry. Editors from some of the biggest fashion magazines had already come up to Jessica expressing their interest in doing an article about the new lingerie line—as well as her partnership with Belle Demoiselle.

That had been the most surprising thing of all . . . the contract that Belle Demoiselle offered to her right after all the untouched photos had been leaked and all the positive attention it had garnered. What had started as Jessica's biggest personal and professional devastation had turned into her greatest triumph. She still couldn't believe all the amazing things that lay ahead for her and Curvy Girl Couture.

"Okay, I'm going to continue my fangirling over there with Maddie," Avery said, pointing to where their friend was also gawking at the celebrity in their midst. "You need to continue mingling since you are the star of tonight's party."

Jessica did just that, very aware that the entire time she circled around the room, conversing with important people, Derek had his eyes on her. He stood off to the side with her brother, Ben, and Asher, who'd brought Nikki for the event. Jason Dare was also with the male group, while his wife, Faith—who'd supplied all the treats for the dessert table and was dressed in one of Jessica's designs—was off perusing the lingerie pieces on display.

She glanced in their direction, and Derek immediately caught her gaze and smiled, the pride in his expression unmistakable. As much as she wanted him by her side, he'd insisted that tonight was *her* night. He was letting her have this once-in-a-lifetime moment to revel in the accolades and enjoy the spotlight.

A few hours passed, and when the party

started to wind down, Jessica made her way to Derek, who was still with Asher and his sister, Nikki. His eyes heated as he took in her subtly sexy cocktail dress, his gaze skimming down the length of her body all the way to her four-inch heels, then slowly back up again. He lingered on her cleavage, and when his eyes met hers, she had to suppress a shiver at the hunger and desire there.

His support over the past few weeks leading up to this night had been incredible. He'd been her rock and made her feel calm and centered, even though her life was currently chaotic. Her love for him had only grown with each day that passed.

She came up to his side, and he slid his arm around her waist and pulled her close, his lips near her ear. "Have I told you lately how fucking amazing you are?"

She smiled and bit her lip. The man was always so full of compliments, something she'd never had in her life, and she loved receiving them from him. "I think it's been at least twenty-four hours."

"Well, you *are* amazing," he reiterated in a low, husky voice meant for only her to hear.

"And beautiful. And so damn sexy I'm dying to get you alone and have you all to myself."

She could feel her cheeks warm.

Standing nearby, Ben frowned at them. "Would you two stop already? We're in a public place, for crying out loud."

"I'm well aware," Derek said with a smirk. "Just letting your sister know how much I adore her."

Ben rolled his eyes. "Who the fuck are you and what have you done with my best friend?"

Derek laughed, and before the two of them could continue their ribbing, Nikki interrupted them.

"Derek . . . I just got a message from Winter Capwell." Nikki stared down at the cellphone in her hand with a frown, referencing the woman who'd recently become a good friend to his sister. "She wants to meet with us to discuss something."

"Me, too?" Derek's dark brows furrowed in confusion. "She's your friend. Why does she want to talk with me?" he asked his sister.

Nikki lifted her gaze to his, looking equally puzzled. "I don't know, but she says it's important, and it pertains to the both of us."

"Weird, but okay," he said with a shrug. "Just not this weekend, because I'm going to be busy with Jessica." He squeezed her hand, making sure she knew she was his priority.

Nikki nodded, then typed a response on her phone. Jessica had no idea what was up with that, either, but figured she'd find out soon enough, right after Derek did.

The after-party ended, Jessica thanked everyone for coming as they left for the evening, then she and Derek headed back to his place in the city. It had only been a few weeks since they'd made their relationship official, but they were already splitting time between his apartment and her house, depending on where they needed or wanted to be. They were essentially living together, and she couldn't be happier about the arrangement.

Once they arrived at his penthouse, Derek disappeared into the main bedroom, and she set her things down on the couch, then walked to the windows overlooking the city. She exhaled a deep breath, a smile on her face as she reflected on just how well the evening had gone.

A short while later, he came up behind her

and wrapped his arms around her waist, bringing her body flush to his. "So, which would you rather . . . have your honeymoon in Florence, Italy, or the Maldives?" he asked, his mouth brushing against her ear as he mentioned two of the places she'd told him she'd like to visit one day.

She turned in his arms, excited about the prospect of traveling with him, but not sure why he was asking about a honeymoon destination. "What are you talking about?"

"*Our* honeymoon," he explained, and she realized she'd missed that part of the question. "After we get married."

The past few weeks had been a whirlwind with Derek, and while they'd solidified their relationship and made a commitment, they hadn't discussed marriage.

Now, as she stared into his serious eyes, she felt a little breathless. "Derek . . ."

He grinned down at her. "I suppose mentioning a honeymoon was a little presumptuous of me. I guess I shouldn't skip the formality of *asking* you to marry me."

A smile twitched at her lips. "No, you shouldn't," she agreed. She wanted the

315

romantic proposal, not just the assumption that they would get engaged.

"All right then," he said and released her.

Reaching into the pocket of his pants, he dropped down to one knee in front of her. His eyes shone with adoration as he opened the black velvet box he held in his hand and revealed a simple but stunning ring, with a heart-shaped diamond in the middle and an intricate design with more sparkling stones around the band. "Jessica Cavanaugh, will you make me the happiest man alive and marry me?"

Her mouth fell open in shock at the ring being in his pocket already, and her heart pounded wildly in her chest. "Derek . . . oh, my God."

He raised his brows. "Should I take that as a yes?"

"Yes!" she replied, tears filling her eyes as she held out her hand toward him. "Oh, my God, *yes*."

He slipped the ring on her finger, then glanced up at her. "This isn't your actual engagement ring. I want us to pick that out together, when you're ready. But in the meantime, this one can be a placeholder, a promise that you and I are in this forever," he said and stood.

"I love it, and I love you." She framed his face in her hands and kissed him, which quickly turned from sweet and soulful to seductive and arousing as Derek's hands began roaming all over her body.

She groaned as he palmed her breast though her dress, her breath hitching with escalating desire.

He lifted his mouth from hers, a wicked little smirk on his lips. "Now, for the more important question . . .would you rather be treated like a good girl tonight or a bad girl once we get into the bedroom?"

His fun, sexy, *which would you rather* questions would never get old. "Which would *you* rather have?"

The sinfully hot glint in his eyes told her that he preferred the latter, even though she knew either way would be fine with him and filled with pleasure. "Why don't you follow me and find out?" he asked and winked at her.

She placed her hand in his and let him lead

her to his bedroom, knowing she'd follow him anywhere.

Thanks for reading! Up next at the bachelor auction: Drew Daniels. (Beck Daniels' brother from JUST ONE SCANDAL by Carly Phillips).

For Book News:
SIGN UP for Carly's Newsletter:
carlyphillips.com/CPNewsletter

SIGN UP for Erika's Newsletter:
geni.us/ErikaWildeNewsletter

Carly Phillips and Erika Wilde Booklist:

A Dare Crossover Series
Just A Little Hookup
Just A Little Secret

Dirty Sexy Series
Dirty Sexy Saint

Dirty Sexy Inked
Dirty Sexy Cuffed
Dirty Sexy Sinner

Book Boyfriend Series
Big Shot
Faking It
Well Built
Rock Solid
The Boyfriend Experience

Made in United States
Orlando, FL
24 March 2023

31386605R00183